Living with Saints

MARY
O'CONNELL

Living with Saints

Atlantic Monthly
New York

ISBN 0-87113-826-3

Atlantic Monthly Press
841 Broadway
New York, NY 10003

Dedication to come

Contents

Living with Saints

Saint Dymphna

Holy shit, thought Dymphna, The Women's Center has hired a moonie. She stared at the walnut name plate on the desk that read "Pamela Craig, Unitarian Chaplain" until the words snapped in her brain, and she remembered that Unitarian meant tambourines and Birkenstocks, not the Reverend Moon marrying 1000 brides to 1000 grooms.

"Dymphna," Pamela Craig said, losing the chummy tone she'd invoked while asking about her Saint Bridget's letter jacket. "I'd like you to tell me how you feel about terminating your pregnancy."

Dymphna said, "Well, of course I feel sad about it."

Pamela Craig nodded.

Dymphna stared up at a poster of a girl kicking an oversized soccer ball. Inside the white spaces on the ball were statistics on low rates of pregnancy and sexually transmitted diseases for teenage girls involved in sports—*outdoor sports*, she thought, enjoying her little joke until she realized she couldn't share it with anyone. Another poster showed a twisted metal clothes hanger spelling the words "Never Again." And then there was a photograph of a naked girl screaming. A cluster of women pinned her to the ground, splaying her arms out, crucifix-style. The caption below the picture explained the girl was about to undergo genital mutilation, as was the custom in rural Somalia. Dymphna wondered what sort of artwhore photographer would document a girl's terror instead of helping her.

Was it the effect of the bullet-proof glaze on the windows, or had dusk really turned the sky a sheer, sugary violet? The air in the small office carried the smell of freshly glazed donuts from the discount bakery next door. When footage of protesters picketing the clinic played on the evening news, there was usually some slacker off to the side, leaning on his sign and eating a long john.

"Why does it make you sad?" Pamela asked.

Dymphna had envisioned The Women's Center as a medical commune, where the staff gave massages, brewed herbal teas and recited poetry. But, no, brisk nurses and doctors shuttled her in and out of exam rooms and finally to this pychobabble torture chamber.

Dymphna said, "Well, it just, you know, isn't a super happy occasion."

She felt teary and fought it, staring into Pamela Craig's plain face, thinking that her pale lashes screamed out for mascara, and she needed cream concealer to smooth out her zit scars.

"Yes, Dymphna, it's a decision that women really struggle with."

"It sure is," Dymphna said, her face blank as a tablet.

"Do you feel guilty about your decision?" Pamela asked.

"I feel terrible," Dymphna blurted. Then she flipped her hair over her shoulder and rallied. "Although I realize it's the best thing for me right now."

"Do you think it's a sin?" Pamela Craig asked.

Dymphna posed dreamily, tucking her hand under her chin. If it wasn't for the green felt cross piercing the B on her letter jacket, if Dymphna had gone to Roosevelt high school, Pamela Craig wouldn't be asking that, and surely equal opportunity laws made her question illegal. And what person under the age of eighty talked about sin?

God *was* ancient and remote, but surely not beyond understanding that she was 17, and had plans to go to the University of Kansas, and then to France, to the Sorbonne for her junior year. *Sorbonne*, she whispered to herself. If she could forgive God, with his noted miracles, for allowing the pregnancy test stick to show two lines, he could certainly forgive her for having an abortion.

"It's not a sin," Pamela Craig muttered.

Why did she answer her own question? Why did this zitty Unitarian think she was queen of the world?

"No offense," Dymphna said, "but, how do *you* know?"

Pamela laughed. "I guess you have a point, Dymphna. And somehow I think you're going to be just fine."

Dymphna knew she'd passed this last hurdle and would be allowed to get her abortion on Saturday morning. Still she wanted to ask one shameful question: How much does an abortion hurt? But Pamela Craig was already leading Dymphna out of her office, saying, oh, she hoped it didn't rain because she hadn't rolled up her car windows and bye-bye, nice meeting you!

Sister Josepha taught Dymphna's first hour class, "Lives of The Saints for Seniors." When she walked into the room carrying her briefcase and a tin of chocolate muffins, all the girls stood up. This was the rule at Saint Bridget's, but most teachers received a wrathful acknowledgment: girls flew up out of their chairs and grinned ironically, or stood with great effort, crossing their arms over their chests, jutting out their hips.

Sister Josepha shooed at them to sit down, and took off her coat and vinyl rain bonnet. Then she walked around the room, placing a muffin and a pink paper napkin on each girl's desk.

Dymphna had just vomited up apple juice and toast in the bathroom, flushing the toilet over and over to mask the sound. She didn't look at the muffin.

"It's such a dreary old day," Sister Josepha said. "I thought we could use a treat." As everyone murmured their gratitude, Kellie Hayes, Dymphna's best friend, put her thumb to her ear and her pinkie to her mouth. She raised her eyebrows wickedly and whispered to Dymphna, "any calls?"

"Oh Jesus," Dymphna whispered, "like if Miles had called, it would be such a minor detail in my fabulous life that I would forget to tell you."

Dymphna met Miles at a college party back in August. After drinking whiskey sours and sharing a joint, they ended up in his pick-up truck, flying along the country roads. Just as Dymphna started to feel the boozy exhilaration of romance, he pulled a spiral notebook from his glove box and flicked on the dome light. He drove with one hand as he recited his poetry, nearly crashing into the railroad crossing signs as he read the line "her breasts, like ivory dinner plates, offered sensual nourishment." To keep from laughing, Dymphna thought of Jesus on the cross, car crashes, and the wise, haggard faces of animals at the pound. But Miles smelled of smoke and bourbon and Ivory soap, and there was the velvet sky and all the blazing white stars.

When Miles pulled off to the side of the road, and whispered, "I would like to make love to you, Dymphna," she whispered, "okay." But as he touched the skin of her back, she grieved: now she was just a body. The talking was over, she'd wasted her opportunities to whisper some tender phrase that would seize him, to tell him she knew Latin and loved Emily Dickinson, that she not just a drunken party girl. In her mind, she rehearsed casual ways of asking him to wear a condom.

"Well, screw him for making you wait by the phone like some seventeenth century maiden, " Kellie said.

Dymphna sighed vigorously. "Of course it's particularly tragic when one considers the myriad ways of using the phone. You can simply dial, or push the number pad with a pencil in your mouth, or hire a miniature monkey. Anyway, I'm not waiting by the phone. Anymore."

Sister Josepha put on her half-glasses and opened her black binder.

"Girls," she said, "after yesterday's marathon of all the Saint Catherines, today we will be discussing the virgin martyrs Saint Cecelia and Saint Dymphna." She lowered her head and grinned at Dymphna. "Now, Cecelia is the patron saint of musicians and poets."

Everything about Sister Josepha—her cigarette-raspy voice, her perpetual cheer, the Lord's wedding band on her thick finger, her purple pantsuit, her adoration of the girl saints, her glamorous, archaic sprayed bubble of gray hair—made Dymphna feel less lonely. But aside from Sister Josepha, some serious rejects taught at Saint Bridget's. Mrs. Hamilton, the English Lit teacher, was hagged out from her divorce and especially vicious to the class beauties. The calculus teacher, young Sister Jeanette, sometimes wept openly about her fanatical love for Our Lord Jesus Christ, but she transformed into a sarcastic bitch if you didn't understand an equation. Occasionally, Dymphna's heart opened to the sorrow of the teachers' lives, like the time she'd seen the lonely, bacheloresque contents of her French teacher's grocery list on his desk: trash bags, hamburger, beer, apples, cheese, peanuts. But that feeling lasted about three seconds because he was such a major pervert. As Dymphna turned away from the desk, she sensed him staring at her butt, and when she snapped her head around to catch him in the act, he blushed a horrible, hammy pink and licked at his handlebar mustache. Even the semi-decent teachers at Saint Bridget's ran pointless film strips while they read novels in the half-light. But with Sister Josepha, class time was an invitation into her world, the world of the saints, and refreshments were served.

"Saint Dymphna was a Celtic virgin martyr," Sister Josepha said. "She is the patron saint of those who suffer from mental illness."

Kellie stabbed her pencil eraser into Dymphna's shoulder blade.

"However, Dymphna herself was not mentally ill. She was the daughter of a pagan king of Ireland whose wife was a devout, gentle Christian. Dymphna enjoyed a happy, carefree childhood growing up in the green fields of Ireland. Though her father had a tyrannical spirit, he doted on his daughter, and her mother loved Dymphna with all her heart. Young Dymphna was a high-spirited girl, known for her kindness. She took her glory in the Lord and pledged her chastity to Jesus Christ."

Dymphna relaxed. She bit into the warm muffin and tasted the kiss of white chocolate melting in the center. If only she could live in this safe room that smelled of clean girls and chalk, if only she could eat chocolate and listen to Sister Josepha and look out the rain-pegged windows forever, she would never have to go to The Women's Clinic on Saturday and get a teeny-tiny baby sucked out of her.

"But Dymphna's peace was short-lived," Sister Josepha said. "Her mother died when Dymphna was only thirteen.

Brutal sadness gripped her soul, and she burned with rage because the Lord had taken her blessed mother. But these feelings subsided, for Dymphna knew she would someday join her mother in heaven. Her father, being a pagan, lived only for the material world and was unable to envision love's paradise, the kingdom of heaven. He wanted to remarry, but he couldn't find another woman as beautiful and kind as his wife, and so he despaired. His evil advisers claimed that the only woman equal to the king's wife was his daughter, Dymphna, and they told him to marry *her*. The king, mad with grief, found this plan ingenious. When he told Dymphna about the wedding plans, she wept for the loss of her mother's protection, her father's madness, and her own sorry circumstances. And then she took action. She sought out her parish priest, and told him of her father's plan. The priest, horrified, as any good person would be," said Sister Josepha, raising her hands to include herself and the girls in this group, "fled Ireland with Dymphna, and they traveled to the town of Gheel, in Belgium. They found solace there for a matter of weeks, until Dymphna's father followed the trail of Irish money and tracked them down in Gheel. He executed the priest on sight. When Dymphna screamed that she would never be his wife, her father plunged his sword into her heart. Now, Dymphna had the sensation of take-off, of her body being lifted by some benevolence and the burdens of our physical world—time, space and gravity—evaporated. She was floating past all her heartache, and she did not rue her life's end, or her father's cruelty. And then, a mystery. Her soul slipped into her father's body and she felt his pain as he watched his daughter dying. Dymphna saw the loneliness her father had known as a boy, and the joy her mother had brought him; she saw he was a weak man, and in looking for a way to erase his sorrow, he'd succumbed to evil. Dymphna died in peace, thanking God for this final mercy, for what could be more precious than to know the true heart of another?"

Sister Josepha closed her binder. "Even now the people of Gheel see the image of Dymphna all over town. In times of trouble her face is etched in the sky. Dymphna Malone, you're lucky to share a name with such a fine saint," she said.

"Thank you, Sister," Dymphna said.

Kellie discreetly kissed her fist.

Dymphna longed to say, Yes, I am an ass-kisser, and what's more, I'm pregnant. But she also wanted to keep her secret. There was no way anyone could find out, unless a maniac walked through the door right now carrying a carton of pregnancy tests and held a gun to each girl's head, forcing her to pee on the test stick and display the results—*My God, Dymphna Malone shows a blue line in the pregnancy window.*

She worried about being kidnapped, held hostage for months, unable to have an abortion. When she emerged from a battered van or a boarded-up house with her stomach round as a melon, people would stare at the TV screen and weep for her tragedy until they ticked the months off on their fingers.

Sister Josepha took off her glasses and wiped them with a lacy blue handkerchief. Then the bell sounded for Calculus class and the world shattered again.

After school she felt too exhausted to change her clothes; she plowed right into bed and dreamed that she peed out a slender baby doll with rhinestone eyes, a pink velvet dress and a long, platinum blonde ponytail. She fished the doll out of the toilet bowl, and went to church, where she sat in the dark confessional stroking the beautiful doll's hair, kissing it.

The priest said, "Dymphna, most pregnant girls have a plastic doll in their uterus."

"Thank you, Father. Thanks for telling me. I was freaked when I thought I had a real baby inside me."

"You poor dear! But you must know the chance of becoming pregnant with an actual human baby is less than ten percent. The girl before you gave birth to Malibu Barbie."

Now the waist band of her skirt cut into her stomach and she did have to pee. She tiptoed into the bathroom and sat on the toilet in the dark.

Through the heat vent she heard her father telling her mother about the sale on dark roast coffee at Foodland, and how delicious the spaghetti sauce smelled—he'd been looking forward to that all day. The water on the stove boiled over so she couldn't hear her mother's reply, just the sing-song cadence of her voice. Her parents kindness and innocence—was it that, or were they morons?—infuriated her.

Back in her bedroom, she clamped on her headphones, not bothering to turn up the ringer on the telephone.

Miles would never call. She thought of praying to Saint Jude, but she'd already prayed for a miscarriage, nine times a day for nine consecutive days, and though this novena had never been known to fail, it failed. Now Dymphna understood that God sometimes said hey, screw you, honey, and stripped the saints of their power. She probably wouldn't even like Miles if he did call. But ever since she'd sat on the edge of the bathtub holding the pregnancy test stick in disbelief, she'd imagined that Miles loved her. During her junior year at the Sorbonne, he would fly to Paris to visit. Even after years of happy marriage, even after having six children, she and Miles would still long for the baby they'd aborted. "But what could we do," Miles would say, "when we were so young?" But first he had to call. First they had to get to know each other.

God! The terror of a baby, of being a moon-faced, visibly pregnant girl slogging down the hallways at Saint Bridget's, before handing her baby over to some happy, worthy couple. Or of living at home with her baby, trapped, watching Barney videos and changing diapers while the world sparkled on without her.

In the end she told Kellie. The two of them sat in Dymphna's Chevy on Saturday morning waiting for their escort into The Women's Center. A security guard with a German Shepard patrolled the parking lot, and the sidewalk leading to the entrance was corded off with red rope. On either side a few de-ranged-looking faces poked out of the crowd, but most people just looked excited.

"What a freakshow," Dymphna said. "It's like the Os-cars."

"Except instead of starfuckers waiting to see celebrities, there's a bunch of losers just hanging around." Kellie lit two cigarettes and handed one to Dymphna.

Jesus, she hoped she could trust Kellie to keep this secret. The power she could lord over her, from this day forward . . .

Kellie pointed to a tall, bearded man in a dark cloth suit holding a bible. "Look," she said, "It's Abraham Lincoln." A pregnant woman stood next to him, and a cluster of children sat at their feet eating sugared donuts. Across the rope, three goateed college-aged guys held round blue signs that read: "Keep Abortion Safe and Legal."

"Check out the three musketeers," Dymphna said. "Why in the hell are they here?"

Kellie said, "My guess is the skin horse brigade want to support their unalienable right not to wear a condom. "

A husky man with a crew cut walked out of the clinic. The word "Escort" blazed across the front of his yellow wind-breaker. People strained over the rope, screaming at him, the cords in their necks popping up like red snakes.

Dymphna took the deepest drag off her cigarette then tossed it out the window and watched it smoke on the pave-ment. Mother of God, if only she could be someone else: fat

Ruth Ann Terrell with her public pledge of virginity, Canada Mulligan, so valiant as she battled leukemia, Susan Rush who wore a bulky metal back brace to correct her scoliosis.

As the escort approached, Kellie said, "That's the guy who takes us in, right?"

"Mmhmm," Dymphna shuddered out.

She grabbed Kellie's hand, which was as shaky and sweat-drenched as her own. Their joined hands draping over the stick shift formed a palsied, wet bird that Dymphna imagined flying through the car window, up, up and away, it's bony finger-wings waving goodbye.

"Oh, Dymphna. It'll all be over by afternoon," Kellie said. "Hey, maybe the doctor will look like George Clooney!"

Dymphna choked out a skittering laugh. "Why in the hell would I want George Clooney to give me an abortion?"

"Oh my God! You are so right! But afterwards, I don't know you, guys could go for coffee and cigarettes, and you could read him your poetry."

Now the man loomed beyond just beyond her car door. As he crouched down, his windbreaker rose up, exposing a gun holster.

If she felt too horrible, afterward, she could always kill herself: Dear *Dr. Kevorkian, though I am not physically ill, it is my wish to leave this world.* God, she thought, I am such a fucking chicken. She unrolled her window.

"Which one of you gals is Dymphna Malone?" His breath smelled like cigarettes and wintergreen lifesavers.

Dymphna put her finger to her chest.

"Okay. I'll need to check your pocketbooks," he said.

As they pushed their purses at him, Dymphna remembered she had maxi-pads in her purse, for afterwards. She stared down at her car mat.

He sifted his hands through their purses without looking inside, then handed them back.

"Okay, girls, once you get out of the car, walk quickly, but don't run. I'll walk in between you, with a hand on each of your shoulders. Now, be warned, people will be yelling all variety of foolishness at you, but keep your heads down and don't make eye contact with anyone. It'll take us about 10 seconds to walk from the car to the doors of the clinic. Ready?"

Dymphna nodded.

"Lock your car doors when you get out. My name's Bud," he said. "I won't let anyone hurt you."

Dymphna stepped out of the car praying for God to deliver her from this. She looked at Bud's cowboy boot's, and at Kellie's rain-stained clogs, and at her own black boots, imagining herself in the future, walking down the street on a happy day, jarred by remembering *these were the boots I wore*. She heard shouting, the honking of a horn, a man singing about Jesus leading us out of darkness, and now, stepping from the asphalt to the concrete sidewalk, a man's voice, close and frightening, speaking about God's will coming down upon fornicators and murderers.

Sorbonne, Dymphna whispered to herself.

It was hard to keep her eyes on the ground. In her peripheral vision she saw Bud's head, raised and defiant, and the snap of Kellie's pony tail against her neck as she walked with her head bowed. An airy, fatigued child's voice asked why, oh why do you like to kill babies, an old woman sobbed into her coffee-colored rosary beads.

A man pushed a large jar over the rope at her, and Dymphna raised her head and saw the pale, mottled baby bobbing beneath the lid. The head was huge and vaguely alien, and the legs floated behind the small body like a tail. Though the baby looked inscrutable as a seahorse floating there in the cloudy liquid, Dymphna felt a rush of love that made her swollen nipples ache.

Bud pushed her head back down. The security guards flung open the metal doors of the clinic.

A nurse led Dymphna down a long hallway from an exam room to the surgical room. Dymphna wore a blue robe, open all the way down the back, with a soft white tie at the throat. She walked with her hand behind her back, pinching the robe shut. They passed Pamela Craig's office, where a girl dabbed her eyes with tissue blackened by mascara, and the doorway to the waiting room, where Kellie sat curled in an orange vinyl chair, drinking soda and reading *People* magazine, haloed by an almost visible crown of smug fortune. Hadn't she slept with eight boys to Dymphna's three?

When Dymphna heard a man's booming voice behind her, she pinched the robe tighter.

"I don't see why I couldn't wear my underwear until I got where I was going," Dymphna snapped.

"Sorry," the nurse said, slapping open the doors to the brightly lit surgical room. She motioned for Dymphna to sit on the beige examining table swathed in white paper, then flashed a mean grin. "The doctor will be right with you, sweetie."

Dymphna lay on the table. She clasped her hands over her chest as if she were lying in a casket waiting for mourners to kiss her cheek.

The doctor walked in, whistling, all hustle and bustle and no greeting. Greasy blond bangs poked out of his green surgical cap. A new nurse flipped though her chart.
"Dymphna," she said, "that's a gorgeous name. Like the saint, right?"

Yes," Dymphna whispered. She shrugged.

It couldn't be possible, but the doctor snorted out a laugh. The nurse stroked the inside of Dymphna's wrist.

"I'm going to need you to scoot way, way down," the doctor said, tapping his hands on the metal stirrups at the end of the table. Dymphna inched down until her hips were at the edge of the table and placed her feet into the cold stirrups. He inserted the cold speculum, proclaiming, "Thiiings are lookin' good."

Dymphna read newspapers; she knew doctors quit working at abortion clinics because people shot them and picketed in front of their houses and followed their children to school.

Abortion clinics had to take any doctor they could get. Dymphna thought of Cindy Duncan, a cross-eyed obese girl in her class who had shown up at the Jubilee Dance with a whippet-thin man in his forties, introducing him to everyone as her 'big sweetie Clifford.'

She gripped the nurse's hand, remembering the photograph of the Somalian girl about to have her clitoris hacked away. Dymphna tried to feel lucky. Immediately she chastised herself for the thought; she'd learned in her Morals and Ethics how wrong it was to take any mercenary pleasure from other people's suffering. Mrs. Louis had paced in front of the chalkboard, smirking. "Let's say you're waiting for that special fellow to call, and as you sit in front of the unringing phone, should you or should you not console yourself by thinking of how Anne Frank felt when the nazis discovered her in the attic?"

Kelly had slipped her a note that read: What makes this bitch think she knows how Anne Frank felt?

"I'm getting ready to deaden the area," the doctor said.

Unbidden, martyred girl saints from Sister Josepha's lectures appeared in her mind—Appalonia who had her teeth wrenched out, and then jumped into flames, Cecelia, suffocated in her bathroom, Agnes, who raised her head to the executioner's sword—all brave, immaculate-hearted, and glorified for their suffering.

When Dymphna walked out of Saint Bridget's on Monday afternoon, she didn't notice the neon green flyer stuck under the windshield of every car in the parking lot; she was looking at the girls around her, thinking how she felt cut away from them now. She'd skipped her morning classes and hidden in a bathroom stall, alarmed by the sludgy blood that wouldn't stop.

"And so ends another riveting day for the young ladies of Saint Bridget's Academy," Kellie said in her Masterpiece Theater voice.

All day Kellie had been trying to cheer her. And over the weekend, she'd called eleven times, breaking up the monotony of cramping and sadness. But now the bleeding had slowed, and Dymphna felt a little better. She looked at the burgundy and gold leaves on the big oak trees and thought about renewal and growth and how she was hungry for an Almond Joy before she glanced at the parking lots and saw neon green flyers on the student cars, and on cars in the first row designated for faculty, and on cars parked in the metered spots along the road in front of Saint Bridget's. Sister Josepha was Monday's parking lot monitor, and she ran willy-nilly through the parking lot, ripping flyers from windshields.

Dymphna spotted her car and ran to it, her thighs aching, her nausea freshened, aware that Nina Kimball and Susan Schultz and Kiera Murphy stood huddling over a flyer, gaping at her as she raced past, aware that the buzz in the parking lot carried her name, aware that Kellie's shoes slapping along the pavement sang out, "Oh shit, oh no, oh shit, oh no."

She slung her backpack on the ground and ripped the flyer from the Chevy's windshield wiper. The grainy, photocopied image showed Dymphna walking into the Women's Clinic. There was her suede coat, the tulip barrette she'd used to keep her long bangs out of her eyes, her black jeans with the rip at the knee, Bud's hand on her shoulder. Visible in the corner was the jar she'd lifted her head to see. Prison bars were stenciled across the photo, and the caption below read:

WANTED FOR THE MURDER OF HER BABY DYMPHNA MALONE

Kellie looked whispered, "Oh my God, Dymphna."

Dymphna stared down at herself.

Most girls stayed frozen next to their cars, though a few walked half-way to Dymphna then stood staring at the pavement, touching their lips, forever caught between compassion and awkwardness.

Dymphna looked at the sky and whispered, "I am at peace because I know the eternal love and forgiveness of our Lord Jesus Christ," but the saint's trick failed her. When Kellie gasped again, Dymphna looked down and saw a slashed baby doll strung to her car bumper with wire.

"Dymphna," Sister Josepha yelled, puffing and huffing from the Marlboros she smoked, her squarish body pounding along with great effort.

Dymphna closed her eyes, trying to shut out this new world, but her brain stuttered with one thought: *Sister Josepha knows I had an abortion on Saturday.* Then she felt the relief of her body being lifted from the ground—an aerial sweetness beyond all measure—and her heart slowed, enjoying the transport. When she opened her eyes, Dymphna saw she was running towards the pale girl with her eyes still clenched shut, holding the flyer which had bled green ink onto her palm. Her lungs ached from the effort of running, and a concrete stiffness clutched her knees. She was in the body of Sister Josepha. It was such a comfort to be delivered that Dymphna did not regret losing her own youthful, fluid movements, nor did it seem strange to have floated away from her physical self. Now the image of a girl standing in the parking lot faded into Sister Josepha's girlhood face—her heavily lashed brown eyes before the crow's feet and eyeglasses, her raven hair in a pixie, her features not yet softened by time and kindness. But Sister Josepha was naked on a kitchen table covered by a blood-stained sheet. She had her legs bent apart, and a man there between them, his fingers inside her. This was a vision, Dymphna knew, and she went further inside, not as the observer, but into the mind of young Sister Josepha. She felt tremors of jerking, hot pain as the sweating man pulled her apart. She looked at the counter and saw a metal bread box and flowered juice glasses drying on the draining board and as she puzzled out the lives of kitchen objects—Did a glass like the warmth of a hand?—Dymphna felt a cutting pain so deep that she shuddered out a scream, and the man working between her legs hissed, "be quiet, you stupid, stupid girl." Now the vision refracted, and Dymphna was both outraged witness, struggling to defend Sister Josepha across time and space, and Sister Josepha herself asking God to let her die.

When Dymphna opened her eyes, she was back in her own body, with Sister Josepha standing in front of her.

"God loves you, Dymphna," Sister Josepha whispered, squeezing her hand so tightly that Dymphna felt the crucifix on her wedding ring. Sister Josepha noticed the doll strung to the car bumper and spat "Bastards!" She cleared her throat, made the sign of the cross and addressed her students: "Girls, let us pray for those evil persons who have perpetuated this act, that they may come to know the true heart of Jesus, which is eternal compassion and love."

The girls of Saint Bridget's bowed their heads in prayer. Dymphna lowered her head in exhaustion though shock still buzzed in her body. A vision: it wasn't like people said in jubilant, showy voices, Christ descending from a splendor of clouds or a blue-robed Mary appearing in back yards, bringing spasms of joy to their Chosen One. Dymphna felt burned away, scarred, sacred and new. Her old ambitions of parties and dorms and Paris vaporized. Now she needed so much more: to live in a world where no one would call her a whore, to be honored, deferred to, feared, adored, to know a transcendent peace that would deliver her from this day. In May she would join the Sisterhood someplace far-off, perhaps the Carmelites in Saint Louis, or the Sister Servants of Mary in California, maybe the Poor Clares in Saulk Rapids, and already she felt a shred of joy that might grow into the exaltation of the risen Christ, already she felt delivered to her new life, as if she watched everything from a safe distance: the parking lot at Saint Bridget's filled with praying girls, Miles, everyone at the Women's Clinic, the people who had decorated the cars with her image, and she was a foreigner now, hovering above them, saying, Fuck you all. I am holy; I am untouchable.

Saint Ursula and Her Maidens

Bands of winter sun filter through the skylight, striping the water with light. The pool's floor is the color of sapphires, a sunken treasure sparkling there beneath the moving water. Descending the staircase at the shallow end, you feel bouyed and cinematic. You are Esther Williams slinking into jeweled blueness until the chlorine stings your eyes. Your friends are already in the pool, floating or stretching. No one speaks. You walk, graceful as a spaceman, the water forcing you up on your toes. Then you raise your stiff feet, and for a second or two, the water holds you.

Edging the pool are bright pink and blue polyeurethane noodles, safety belts, ankle and wrist supports, hand paddles, flippers and inflatable rings for children. A canvas hammock dangles from chains tethered to a steel pole. The hammock is for people unable to use the stairs; physical therapists help them into the hammock, then lower them into the water.

The Ursuline sisters run the community center, and on the wall next to the pool rules hangs a bronze plaque depicting Saint Ursula and her maidens aboard a ship, with a short hagiography. Ursula was a fourth-century British princess betrothed to the son of a pagan King. To delay her unwanted marriage, Ursula asked permission to sail the seas for three years with eleven thousand virgin companions. At the end of this grace period, when sailing off the shores of Cologne, they were massacred by the Huns because of their devotion to Christ. And so Ursula triumphed. Jesus was her only lover; she was never a land-locked, bitter bride.

Today's water therapy teacher stands at the side of the pool doing deep knee-bends. She is perhaps fifty, in a navy swimming suit and red flip-flops, thin except for the heavily veined cellulite clumping her thighs. The teachers come and go. Most are college girls working toward physical-therapy degrees. Before class, they apply frosty lip gloss and watch the TV suspended from the ceiling. They never actually enter the pool, preferring to yell their instructions from the side because chlorine is bad for their highlighted, butter-blonde hair. You, who paid sixty dollars for a garnet-brown rinse to color your creeping strands of gray, fully experience the ravages of chlorinated water.

You move your weight from foot to foot. The water muffles the popping of your hips. You are thirty and arthritic. Two years ago when your fingers and toes started to hurt, you thought, *This is a strange flu,* and then you thought: *Arthritis. Well I've always been mature for my age, ha ha.* Then your hands stiffened into claws and your knees locked and would not straighten. The doctors said chronic rheumatoid arthritis which made you think of nursing home cronies, hunched over, playing gin rummy. Then you got sicker, and you started hearing stories: *My cousin ended up in a wheelchair after only three years . . . The lady down the block has hands like pretzels . . . My stepfather's knees are fused and guess what he walks like Frankenstein.*

As you wave your hands through the water, the stony heaviness in your fingers starts to subside. There is a big, witchy nodule in your wedding ring finger and one developing in your pinkie. You plunge your hands deeper, slide them across your stomach.

You have a zygote. Zoe Zachary Zygote, your husband calls it, and the world is muzzy and mint-green, soft as lamb's ear. And your health is much improved. After all those dark days you have suddenly plunged into Candyland. The trees blossom with caramel apples; the sun shines it's creamsicle rays especially for you.

Of course you worry, the word "chronic" embossed in your brain in fright-show letters. Will you backtrack into full-time convalescence? Will you be able to screw the nipple on a baby bottle?

The teacher crashes into the pool and shouts "Let's warm up by walking across the pool and back five times."

The water makes walking a snap. You wish for a sudden season of monsoons. With rainwater to your waist, you could race though the grocery store parking lot like the track star you were in junior high.

There are just five women in the slow movement class. Marjorie—a retired nurse, now an Avon lady—is the oldest at sixty-five. Or is Sister Barbara, an Ursuline sister who lives in the run-down convent visible through the windows? She hasn't offered up an exact number, a vanity that charms you.

"This methotrexate makes my mouth so damn dry, I could spit cotton," Marjorie says. "I'd love an ice-cold beer."

Sister Barbara cups water in her hands. "According to legend," she tells you, "Saint Ursula transformed great buckets of ocean water into beer. Imagine the fantastic parties she and the maidens had on deck! Imagine all the water in this pool transformed into golden, sparkling Michelob."

You lower your mouth to lap at the air just above the water like a cat.

Carlin says, "I'd like a pool filled with Chardonnay and chocolate."

Carlin is in her early thirties. She is in the Junior League and has a Range Rover and two children and an orthopedic-surgeon husband and multiple sclerosis.

"I'll pass," Marjorie says. "Do you know the number of catheter bags that leak in this pool all day? I wouldn't drink from this pool if it were filled with champagne. And let's not even talk about floating chocolate."

Sister Barbara cracks up, and you laugh weakly, a new nausea fluttering your throat. Carlin mouths the word *bad* then laughs.

Marjorie and Sister Barbara can barely contain themselves. They both have lupus and call themselves "the luscious lupus twins." Lupus can be deadly, but to you it sounds like a purple cone-shaped flower: On a fresh spring day I went strolling through a field of heather and lupus. On top of having lupus Marjorie has ovarian cancer. Apparently, the chemotherapy has sent her lupus into remission. ("A miracle cure," says Marjorie.)

Heather, the baby of the group at 19, walks across the pool with her head down, sullen. This has not gone unnoticed but you don't badger each other.

"Leg stretches," the teacher yells.

You all line up next to the chrome handrail jutting from the side of the pool. Grasping the bar with one hurting hand, you raise your left leg to the side, to the front, to the side, to the front.

Heather exhales loudly.

"What is it, hon?" Marjorie says, her many-shaded eyes squinting into rainbows of concern.

Heather wipes a tear away with her raw-knuckled hand. "Just look at my face. It's huge! Jesus, how I hate Prednisone."

Prednisone is a steroid that suppresses the immune system. Also, it causes severe mood swings, weight gain, acne, and, in an interesting twist, gives you lustrous facial hair while causing hair loss of the scalp. Worst of all is Heather's current problem, Cushings syndrome, a steroid-induced-moon face.

"Leg stretches," the teacher calls.

You lift your right leg too high and wonder if a zygote gets dizzy. Zygote—the most beautiful of all medical terms. Actually, speeded by the wonders of time and cell division, your zygote transformed, first to an embryo, and now to its current incarnation as a fetus. You are eleven weeks pregnant and sentimental, unable to give up the term "zygote," the miracle of that first primitive cell.

Heather goes on: "My bitchy doctor said, 'well, if Prednisone makes it more comfortable for you to walk around, what's the problem? Is a bloated face worse than losing your mobility?'"

"Oh Heather, she sounds like a royal bitch," says Marjorie.

"No lie," you say.

"I'll tell you what, those damn doctors love to prescribe that nasty old Prednisone." Sister Barbara says.

"My husband isn't as pro-Prednisone since he had to live with me while I was taking it," says Carlin. "But he did say it was nice not to see me dragging my ass around the house like I was ninety-five years old."

"Wave goodbye with your foot," the teacher calls out.

Carlin sings softly, "I don't know why you say goodbye, I say hello."

"What I felt like saying," says Heather, "was, 'Well of course you wouldn't understand how seeing your face swell up like a blowfish would be a drag, Doctor Hagula; you're not even *pretty*.' I'm going to call her and tell her that. I mean, God, I'm a freaking medical anomaly. What else could possibly go wrong? And I'm getting a fat body to match my pumpkin head. With Crohn's disease you're supposed to be stick thin. If I could be sick and fabulously skinny that would be another thing altogether."

Carlin sinks in her cheeks and lets her eyelids droop. "Bring on the heroin chic look."

"Well, they say chemo makes you too nauseous too eat, " Marjorie says, "but I stopped for a banana split on my way home yesterday."

"Don't talk to me," Sister Barbara says, "I ate an entire box of chocolate-covered cherries last night while I was watching TV last night and woke up at 2 A.M. with the sugar sweats."

"Let's pick up the pace, ladies," the teacher yells, slapping her hips. "Let's stretch out that lower body!"

You sway like an elderly hula girl. On the soundless TV, a group of girls play soccer while one small girl looks on from the sidelines.

"Jesus Christ," Heather says, "I hate these commercials. 'You can give a girl a ball or you can give a girl a doll.' Is that Nike's version of feminism?"

Carlin grins at you. On her swimming suit is the famous swoosh. Beneath the water, you wear Nike pool shoes.

Sister Barbara says, "I love the Tiger Woods commercials, though."

Heather slaps the water. "Oh Sister Barbara, I hate those so much. Sure, they have all those cute little kids looking into the camera, saying, 'I am Tiger Woods.' Of course they never show the Indonesian children who sew Nike shoes in sweat shops for a dime an hour. I guess their sport is sewing.'"

"I'm wondering why they keep the TV on in here," Marjorie says.

Sister Barbara reaches out and touches Heather's hand. "Sweetheart, how many milligrams of the Prednisone do they have you on?"

You, too, have become outraged by commercials and magazine stories; you write letters to editors and rage about pesticides and the sodium content of canned soup. Before illness, you were easygoing and charitable. Now it's clear that your previous good works—all that prancing around like Mother Theresa with eyeliner—only disguised your innate evil. When you were at your worst, people would say, *Gee, I'm so busy. I really envy you being able to stay home and watch TV all day.* How you wanted them killed, how you wanted their remains to serve as evidence of the grotesquerie of their deaths—severed heads shellacked and forever stuck on a stick in some psychopath's closet. *Gee, maybe in the next life you'll have time to watch TV.* But now you have a zygote and everywhere people in their tenderness are too much for you to bear: the old woman at the drug store struggling to work the blood-pressure cuff, the fat boy walking his teacup poodle in the rain.

"Move like you mean it!" the instructor shrieks.

"For the love of God," Sister Barbara says, "does she think she's teaching the hydro-crunch class? Doesn't she know we're the slow girls?"

To improve coordination and muscle tone, you each strap on hand paddles. The velcro straps scritch-scritch and now, under water, your hands are as leaden and clumsy as they are on land.

"Arm Circles!" The instructor yells.

Your shoulders creak. You windmill your arms lethargically. Inside you is a zygote; you'll never walk alone.

Carlin jerks back into the water, coughing, her hands slapping the surface, her long black hair wet and gleaming, sloping like a stole over her tanned shoulders. There is a slow second in which you each lunge toward her before she stands upright, sputtering, "I'm okay, I'm okay."

"Oh, hon," Sister Barbara says. She unstraps her hand paddles and tosses them to the side of the pool, then pats Carlin on the back.

Carlin coughs and laughs in the same breath. "Geez, Sister Barbara, anything to lose those water weights, huh?"

"You got it, girl," says Sister Barbara.

The teacher blows her silver whistle. "Miss, are you okay? Can you breathe, speak or cough?"

Marjorie whispers, "Isn't that what you say when someone is gagging on a pork chop?"

"I'm fine," Carlin says.

The teacher taps her finger on the whistle and looks away.

"Are you sure you're okay?" you ask.

"I'll live. Anyway, that's what I get for being Miss Sissy Girl and staying in the shallow end so my hair wouldn't get wet." Then she loses the smile and her shoulders sink. "My balance is terrible today. I almost couldn't drive because the streets looked so wavy. God."

Heather says, "On the other hand, even wet, your lipstick still looks perfect."

Carlin waves at Heather like the Queen Mother. "I've been in a flare for about two weeks now. I started feeling awful right after my high school reunion, which I went to because I'm a moron. Everyone who didn't know I had MS was sort of grudgingly nice to Brad and me, because high school is never really over, and everyone hopes that the homecoming queen will turn into the Goodyear Blimp or whatever, but, as it turns out, I've given them so much more. You could tell the people who knew I had MS, because they'd say, *Oh Carlin*, with this delicious smile on their face. I was in the bathroom and I heard these two bitches in the other stalls talking: *It's so sad that she'll go blind, isn't it? By our next reunion she'll probably be in a nursing home. Poor Carlin, I bet she'll end up crippled, with lots and lots of bedsores. Oh, isn't it terrible? Let's not talk about this, it's so darn depressing.* It was like they'd won the lottery."

Sister Barbara nods. "People who aren't happy with their own lives feast on the troubles of others."

You decide to homeschool your zygote, preferably in the wilderness, to avoid high school and it's aftershocks.

Carlin closes her eyes and lifts her head to the sun cutting through the skylight. "It's funny, though. As the night went on, and the gossip about me spread, I could feel the mood in the room change. People kept comparing their lives to what they imagined my life was like, and believing they were winning in a big way. I felt their joy at my fate. I have never, ever felt more powerful, and I'm pretty sure it's how Jesus must have felt at The Last Supper when he said, 'This is my body, which will be given up for you.'"

Everyone stares into the water.

"Anyway, that feeling didn't last. On the drive home I wanted to stop and buy a pistol. If it wasn't for my kids I would have blown my brains out the day I was diagnosed."

Marjorie says, "you know, last night I was watching Francis at the dinner table, eating his chicken breast and baked potatoes, and maybe we've eaten a million meals together, and I've never given it a second thought. But as I watched him chew his chicken, I thought maybe I'd sneak up behind him and shoot him with his hunting rifle, so he'd never have to eat dinner alone, and I could stop worrying about him being lonely when I'm gone."

"Oh, you guys," Heather says. "I've been wanting to shoot myself all week."

The instructor claps her hand together. "Ladies!" she says, "we need to get back to our exercise! Don't be such a group of sad sacks! Remember, when we feel tempted to indulge in self-pity, we must think of others who are less fortunate."

"Saint Ursula, help us, " Sister Barbara says.

Right on cue, the locker-room door slams shut, unaided; in the next world, Saint Ursula and her maidens are slamming down their beer mugs in disgust.

The teacher smiles dreamily. "Think of Christopher Reeve. Superman sits strapped in a chair, all day, completely helpless. Why, he can't lift a spoon. I saw him on TV the other night, and though he can't move a muscle, he still has zest for life. We can all learn a lesson from his courage."

"Excuse me, Miss," Sister Barbara says.

That 'Miss' sounds awfully righteous, partly because the teacher's age qualifies her to be a ma'am. And maybe the teacher mistakes Sister Barbara for a dotty old woman with a gray bubble cut and a flowered lavender swimsuit, because she turns and grins like she's about to be offered a plate of brownies and says, "Yes?"

"It is not right," Sister Barbara says, "to use the misfortune of others to cheer ourselves. It is an insult to Christopher Reeve that his recent tragedy would be used as a catalyst to brighten people's lives. You can be quite sure that your pity is of no use to Christopher Reeve. You can be quite sure that in the eyes of God, the greatest sin is gleeful, self-congratulatory compassion."

You wonder why you ever switched over to the Unitarians. The whole idea of a peaceful God sucks. How you miss your old Catholic God, capable of eternally punishing people who acted like assholes while on earth. Then again, the Unitarian God might be a slacker, but he/she is kind and loving, while the Catholic God is such a stormy friend. But you don't want God concocting any schemes to punish your zygote for your own murky thoughts so you block them out—Gloria in Excelsius Deo.

The teacher is still smiling at Sister Barbara, but in a dazed, frightened way. She suddenly remembers a dental appointment and tells everyone to exercise at her own pace. You cruelly freeze your eyes on her flapping hips as she rushes to the locker room.

Sister Barbara asks, "Did I come on too strong? No one likes a bully."

Saint Ursula and her maidens received a three year reprieve from the struggles of life on land but you only get an hour on Tuesdays and Thursdays.

There's five minutes of pool time left when a male water therapist screams and fake-falls into the deep end, Jerry Lewis-style. He bobs up, gasping, and waves wildly to a little girl in a red, ruffled bathing suit. The girl parks her silver walker by the pool stairs. Robin's egg-sized muscles pop out of her upper arms and her sandy blonde hair is in a ribboned French braid. She sits on the first step and the water therapist walks to her, Godzilla-like, growling, with his arms raised over his head. Then he scoops the little girl into his arms so gently that their movement looks like slow motion. She squeals as he puts a safety ring around her. Beneath the water, her legs are a secret. The therapist pulls her around, their heads pressed together, and she answers his questions seriously, with a lisp.

You concentrate on Marjorie and Sister Barbara's conversation—Penney's has a half-off sale on support bras; will they have just one cup?—and their laughter. But in your peripheral vision is the miniature silver walker, shiny as a tin star, decorated with Hello Kitty stickers. The therapist throws the girl a sponge basketball, and they take turns dunking it in the mesh basket at the side of the pool.

"Two points, Tiffany!" says the girl's mother, who stands at the side of the pool, clapping.

You decide that your zygote is healthy, that your own illness has served as insurance for the well-being of your baby—if only you could get that policy. Then you glance at the silver walker and pray, *Please God, anything but that, tear me to shreds, bring it on, but please, please, please not that.*

Tiffany misses a long shot and the sponge basketball smacks you in the shoulder. As you lob it back, you offer her a phony, neutral smile. This is the kind of person you are now, praying for protection against this beautiful child, worried that she will place a sort of osmotic hex upon your zygote. This is the sum total of wisdom you've gained from your illness.

Sister Barbara looks at you. "You've been quiet as a church mouse today."

Heather says, "Yeah, what gives?"

You feel the heat of tears behind your eyes, your lips twitching and fluttering like a pageant winner. Tell them you saw two blue lines on a stick.

You are a celebrity.

In the locker room, everyone sits down on the long wooden bench and peels off her bathing suits. You take great care to only look at each other above the neck as you step into the group shower. Usually, hot water bursts out of the tiny metal heads with such force it feels as if you're being blasted with a pellet gun, but today the flow is like rain drops.

Heather and Sister Barbara gaze at you like you're the Virgin Mary. Marjorie tells you that thirty is the perfect age to have a baby; that's how old she was when she had Timmy, the last of her six children. As she reaches up to turn off the shower nozzle, she gives you a toothy, devastating smile. "You'll be a fun mom," Marjorie says.

The world is lit by pink and blue birthday candles. Your heart is a three-tiered white-frosted cake studded with Junior Mints.

In the dressing room, you contribute your part in the chorus of popping toes and knees. Your shoulders clench as you bend down to step into your underwear, but, my God, you have a zygote!

Carlin tells a story of how, shortly after she was diagnosed, she was at the mall, sitting on a bench giving her baby Katherine a bottle, when two women wearing shapeless peasant dresses and Birkenstocks walked past her, glaring. The women circled back to tell her that the "breast is best," and that she was probably poisoning her baby by feeding her formula. Then gave her a pamphlet from the La Leche League.

"I told them the medicine I took for the MS would transfer through my breast milk and kill my baby," Carlin says. "I really let them have it. Those hippie bitches were in tears by the time I was through with them." She hooks her black bra and pulls her shirt over her head, then vamps in front of the fogged mirror. "And the moral of this little story is that because I couldn't breast feed, my tits are still riding high."

"God, to have your tits riding high is the best moral of any story," you say.

Marjorie and Sister Barbara agree that, at their age they couldn't achieve the same look with a bra made of steel.

No one really wants to leave, but you all put on your rubber-soled shoes and walk carefully out the door. The cold stiffens your fingers to iron bars. Sand grits most of the sidewalk, but here and there are patches of gleaming, bare ice.

Sister Barbara loops her arm through yours and says, "Careful there, Mom"—which is so ridiculous: your "baby" could ride in Jiminy Cricket's backpack; it could swim laps in a dessert spoon. Still, you probably don't need your cold car today. You could probably fly home.

At the edge of the parking lot Marjorie stops and says, "I've got the new Avon catalogs in the car, would you all like to sneak a peek before you head home?"

The slow movement group piles into her tanklike green Mercury. Your breath forms a pulsing cloud as Marjorie sticks a catalog into your gloved hand. The light snow powdering the car windows shields you from the outside world but you hear the roar of cars on the highway. Soon, you'll be driving on that highway, but not quite yet.

In the front seat Sister Barbara traces her finger over a palette of pale lipstick colors. Snuggled up to you on the left, Carlin is looking at alpha-hydroxy creams. On your right, Heather frowns at a page of mascaras.

"My roommates are all rockhounds," she says, "but I'm not even sure if I want to get married. My hands are so shaky, I'd rather hook up with a nice drag queen who could apply my mascara without stabbing me in the eye."

"Who wouldn't?" Carlin says. "But it would never work, all the women would be chasing after him, wanting him to line their lips, their eyes, begging for it."

Marjorie says "Isn't is strange? Young women of my generation didn't wear much makeup, just lipstick and powder," but Sister Barbara says, "speak for yourself, hon. I never left the house without my false eyelashes." Marjorie puts on the wipers to clear the windshield and you see a winter bird perched on a stop sign, a man's dark glove in the snowy parking lot, and the car heater kicks in, moaning, not yet, not yet.

Saint Therese of Lisieux

Sister Beth calls out my name, "Kendra Murphy," then pauses for dramatic effect before saying, "Therese of Lisieux," the last syllable a sensual *syuuu*. The winter sun cutting through the blinds carves three diamonds on my desk as she pinches a bloom from her prized miniature rosebuds on the windowsill and lobs it to me in the back-row, blushing, saying "A little flower for the little flower." I catch the rose and smile back at Sister Beth. But when she turns her back, I crunch it up in my hand and stick my finger down my throat. My beauty is a gift from God, and standardized tests revealed me as a near-genius, but popularity requires a certain amount of panache. And you might think Sister Beth would show a drop of imagination and not give me the star assignment, the hagiography of our school's namesake, Therese of Lisieux, the little flower. I'd prefer an obscure, forgotten saint, say Christina the Astonishing, an insane girl who couldn't tolerate the smell of human skin and prayed for her death. But Sister Beth assigns Saint Christina to Jenna Kellerman the Wacko, who spent a week recuperating at Four Oaks hospital after her latest suicide attempt. Anna Platt, flute virtuoso, is given Cecelia, patron saint of musicians; Stacey Ramos, my best friend, is given a Hispanic saint, Saint Rose of Lima, and so on, until everyone is assigned their hagiography and we're excused to research our saints in the library.

On the way out of class I toss the rose in the metal trash can. And then, for no reason, I have a moment of giddy happiness. My heart flips in my chest as we walk down Saint Therese's main hallway, which will be demolished over the summer so we won't croak from the asbestos dust and flaking lead paint. The window moldings are scrolled with roses, crosses, ornate Latin calligraphy and trumpeting, soft-eyed angels. I bring my hand to my face to cover a cough and smell the faint sweetness of the rose.

After school the suburban mothers roar into the big circle drive in front of Therese of Lisieux in sport utility vehicles. The girls climbing into their bulky, sparkling cars look humiliated, like they wished they lived downtown and could walk home like Stacey and me. We offer them mournful smiles as they pull away.

"I got jacked," I tell Stacey.

"How so?" she asks.

My backpack is falling, too heavy with books about Saint Therese, and I tug on the shoulder straps as we cut through the icy drive. We wear parkas, chunky-soled snow boots, and thick leggings layered beneath our uniforms. Our knit hats are jammed in with our books; it's not that cold.

"Therese of Lisieux is an idiot. A rich bitch who lived in a mansion and received a special audience with the pope to get permission to join the convent at 15. Oh, and she wanted a shower of roses to fall from heaven when she died, which is so Hallmark queer. And she always, always wanted to be a saint. It was a goal. Which should totally disqualify you."

"God, how embarrassing to have our school named after some ass-kissing dork," Stacey says, her breath a cold cloud. "But how about Sister Beth assigning me a Hispanic saint? She thought, hmmm, perhaps the Mexican girl would enjoy partaking in the cultural heritage of Saint Rose of Lima?"

"Oh my God, that cracked me up."

Snow flakes land on Stacey's glossy black hair and long eyelashes, clinging there for a fast second before they melt to water drops.

"I guess there aren't any black saints—because that crazy Klansman Jesus only loves white people—or surely Sister Beth would have assigned one to Darcy Thurston. By the way, Saint Rose of Lima is a real winner, too. She rubbed lye and hot pepper into her face to burn away her beauty. Shouldn't a saint be working for the poor or whatever instead of doing reverse-beauty masks?"

"Stacey, but do you remember when you bleached your sideburns and left the cream on too long and burned *your* face?"

"Bitch from Hell! I can't believe you would bring that up."

"It wouldn't be funny if the bleach had scarred you. But it seems to me that you're Saint Rose of Lima incarnate." I mock-shiver, chattering my teeth. "It's uncanny."

She gives me the finger, but she's laughing and saying, my, my, what a coincidence, that I'm an ass-kissing freak like Therese of Lisieux, and I'm calling her Our Lady of Jolene Cream Bleach as we walk down eighteenth street where the city buses blast us with fumes, and cars crammed with boys honk and catcall, and I wish we lived miles and miles away and could walk through the snow all night, but already we are turning onto Meridian, already there is Stacey's house on the corner, and further down the street, mine.

"Come on in," Stacey says, heading up the walk to her door.

I stand at the end of the walk, dragging one boot through the snow in a half-circle.

"Ten minutes won't matter that much," Stacey says, and I follow her inside.

We shed our coats and boots as Mrs. Ramos waves hello, hello, her nails gleaming geranium-red, her diamond wedding band flashing, and she cradles her arm around me, leading me into the kitchen, the brief heaven of her Chanel no. 5 and warm body making me lightheaded. The eight-year old twins, Paige and Esmerelda, are at the kitchen table eating cake and staring up at the TV on the counter. "Hi Kendra," they say in unison, then grimace, burdened by identical cuteness. Stacey's older sister Jennifer, a senior at Saint Therese, is stretched out on the floor talking on the portable phone and sporadically pounding her feet on the linoleum, laughing.

Stacey and I sit down, and without asking, Mrs. Ramos brings us each a piece of warm vanilla cake and tall glasses of milk. Being here in the Ramos' kitchen—the fresh daisies in a silver pitcher on the table, the thrumming heat from the floor vents warming my cold feet—is like smoking pot: the sweet, woozy feeling destroyed by flashes of jumpy anxiety: Why am I here? A car chugs down the alley and Mrs. Ramos looks out the window over the kitchen sink and smiles. Mr. Ramos is home now, whistling as he walks in the back door. Whistling! He kisses the twins on the forehead then kisses Stacey on the forehead before he shakes my hand gently. Here is a man who would never pull you into a hearty, tit-crushing hug. He acts like he's going to lean down and kiss Jennifer before he rubs his lower back comically and blows her a kiss. Mrs. Ramos takes his coat and they kiss quickly on the lips.

I eat a few more bites of cake, but I still feel the perfect gentleness of Mr. Ramos hand in mine.

I excuse myself to go to the spotless, apple-green bathroom where I sit on the toilet, pull back the shower curtain and examine the immaculate tub. I swear, even the rust spots circling the drain are buffed to a shine. On the window sill an apple-green ceramic pot holds white flowers blooming out of onion-like bulbs. I quit peeing mid-stream, place the flowers down between my legs, and pee again, soaking the soil and splattering the ceramic pot. I put it back on the sill and flush the toilet. There is a palette of fruit-scented lip gloss on the bathroom counter and I drag my finger through the banana and the soft pink watermelon, then smear the mixture, along with a rind of dirt from under my thumbnail, into a contact lens dispenser. Then I open the drawer beneath the sink and rummage through the cosmetics, spitting into a bottle of foundation, running a velour powder puff over the toilet seat, flushing an eye shadow applicator down the toilet.

Finally I make sure everything is in order, wash my hands, drag a brush through my hair and sample a ruby red lipstick, Roses in the Snow. There is a stack of pastel wash cloths and towels in a white wicker basket next to the tub and I blast them with air freshener—apple potpourri—before I leave.

I walk down the block reading Saint Therese's autobiography, "The Story of a Soul." Occasionally it reads like a Harlequin novel for nuns, pure crap about how God loves the flowers in the field, but I'm warming to it when a tiny old man in a station wagon rolls down his window to call out, "que hermosa, que hermosa," in a frail, beyond-the-grave voice.

I never have privacy.

Though I scrubbed my hands at the Ramos' house, the smell of Sister Beth's rose, cold and sweet, rises up through my gloves as I read. Saint Therese's Father called her his "little queen." Of his five daughters, she was his favorite. Also, he preferred Therese to his wife.

The shades are drawn and the TV muted, silencing the Teletubbies. Mom is on the couch, curled up with baby Caroline in a flowered sling on her chest. Xavier stands up in the playpen, his fat little hands knotting the mesh sides, crying out, "Tendra, Tendra."

"Oh Kendra, you're home," Mom says.

"Yep." I raise Xavier over my head. His diaper is soaked, heavy as paper mache.

"I guess he needs to be changed," she says.

She is depressed, but too look at her you would certainly guess: crack addict. Her black hair is matted in greasy curls and her face looks too thin, with purple-gray shadows ringing her eyes and a weird rash spangling her cheeks. If she's even wearing a bra she forgot to put in the cotton nursing pads; the front of Dad's old striped shirt is drenched with jagged rectangles of breast milk.

I fish out Xavier's bottle from the jumble of toys in the playpen. It is sucked dry with the nipple still indented.

"He just finished that," Mom says quickly "He just took the very last drink."

Caroline wakes, crying softly, as if heartbroken. Mom unbuttons her soggy shirt and nurses her.

I carry Xavier into the kitchen, where the sink overflows with sticky breakfast dishes and pans from last night's chicken dinner. Tonight will be a pizza night. In the refrigerator is the gigantic jug of 10% real fruit juice that Dad purchased at The Price Chopper. As I fill Xavier's bottle he waves his hands over his head, thrilled.

Upstairs in the babies' room, I change his diaper, then rock him while he guzzles his bottle and dozes off, his sweet, juicy breath warming my neck. There are only three diapers left in his box and not many more of the tiny diapers my sister wears.

When I compare our dirty bathroom to the Ramos' scrubbed shrine it makes my front teeth ache, but I steal a half-hour before dinner to take a bath and read. In "The Story of a Soul" Therese alludes to her great beauty, but in photographs from other library books, she is quite the dog. Therese's mother dies when she is five. Two of her older sisters leave the family to join the Carmelite Nuns, and despite her love and faith in Jesus, young Therese is bereft. She is smart, but not well liked at school. She cries during her lessons and, on the playground, gazes piously up at the heavens. She prays to join the Carmelites, to live forever cloistered from the world with her sisters, to make herself over, small and humble, a little flower plucked by Jesus.

Dad massages my shoulders while I stand at the sink washing dishes. Mom is feeding Xavier a jar of sweet potatoes, and he slaps the tray on his high chair and twists his head from side to side, performing an infant crazy-from-the-waist-up boogie while he eats. Caroline is already asleep. No bath for her. Tomorrow night is a must.

As Dad lifts up my hair and rubs my neck, I turn the water faucet hotter and watch my hands redden beneath the suds. Mom looks up at us, as if from another galaxy, then stirs the sweet potatoes, the baby spoon ringing around the jar.

"Everyone in the office saw your name in the paper for winning the Francis of Assisi humanities scholarship. And they know you're only a sophomore," Dad says.

"Great."

"Of course they have only the vaguest notion of what the humanities are. Anyway, my sorry-ass cubicle has so many pictures of you from the newspaper, I'm starting to look like a stalker."

"Dad, will you put the pizza box in the recycling bin?"

He takes his hands off my back and clicks his heels together, saluting me.

I escape to the basement to do a couple loads of laundry, and when I come back upstairs, Dad is watching TV and Mom is already in bed though it's only 8:15. I know she's tired from caring for a three-month old and a fourteen-month old all day. I understand everything.

In my room I solve calculus problems, feeling calmer as I space the numbers and letters between blue lines of notebook paper. When David LaFrael calls and asks me to go to the movies, I'm not even tempted.

"You haven't told anyone about my mother, have you," I whisper into the phone, smelling Dad's sour breath on the receiver

"No," he says, disgusted. "You asked me not to. But it's nothing to be ashamed of."

David escorted me to the homecoming game where I was crowned sophomore princess, tah-dah, and later that night, with the seventies retro band blaring from the gym, we made out in a bathroom stall at Saint Therese. When he put his hand on my breast, I had a made-for-TV-movie breakdown and started to cry. Then I said, "My mother has breast cancer," and he was sweetly concerned and full of helpful advice. His father, as it turns out, is an oncologist. Why does Jesus hate me? As I stood pressed up against the sanitary napkin disposal he asked questions about her course of treatment—chemotherapy? tamoxifen?—until I wanted to pierce his eyeballs with my corsage pin.

I crawl into bed, snuggle down, and read "The Story of a Soul." Dad comes into my bedroom and looks out the window, where snowflakes feathering the glass are the silver-white of Marilyn Monroe's hair.

"Snow was general all over Ireland," Dad says softly. "Do you know what that's from, Kendra?"

"Sure do," I say.

I keep reading; I am a speed reader. When Therese goes to Italy to plead with the pope to let her enter Carmel, she alludes to something strange happening on the journey, saying, "Let us pray for the bad priests!" A curious comment.

Dad pulls the shade on the new snow and lays down on the bed next to me, yawning.

Could Therese have known a bad priest like Father Sam? Suzette King was planting crocus bulbs outside of the rectory at Saint Therese of Lisieux when Father Sam invited her in for "a nice glass of cola." They ended up having sex on the living room couch beneath an oil painting of a moon-faced, mournful Jesus. Palm fronds from years of Palm Sunday masses were stuck behind the painting, and they scattered down on the naked bodies of Suzette and Father Sam. To Suzette, it looked like God was lashing Father Sam with dried-up yellow whips. This added greatly to the otherworldiness of the experience, the basic reason Suzette was doing it in the first place. Afterwards, Father Sam fixed her a box of macaroni and cheese, the cheap brand that doesn't get very yellow, and cried into his ironed handkerchief.

Father Thomas, the older parish priest at Therese of Lisieux, has never, to my knowledge, invited anyone in for a nice glass of cola. Even with his lisp and cracked brown teeth, I sometimes fantasize that Father Thomas is my real father. During confession he told Mom to get some Prozac so she could take better care of the babies. Dad said: Well, golly, I wasn't aware he was a doctor.

Now Dad strokes my arm. I put down my book and pull my nightgown over my head so I don't have to suffer through Dad unbuttoning it with his teeth and whispering sweet nothings like some eighteenth century-lover, and we have sex, him on top of me, me staring up at the ceiling, then looking at the digital clock, steeling myself against the moment where I feel myself shivering and breaking with dad gasping "that's right," in my ear, steeling myself against the moment where he is walking back down the hall and I'm in the bathroom peeing and cleaning up and thinking of things other people in the world might be doing right now—sometimes the Ramos's pop pop-corn and make a kettle of hot cocoa and sit around the kitchen talking late, even on school nights.

First hour on Friday is devoted to The Social Experience. Some loser visits our class to explain The Bad Thing That Has Happened To Me And How It Has Made Me A Stronger Person. Today the loser is a woman who was molested in her youth. Oh, joy. Everyone in class looks bored—they've heard this discussed a trillion times on afternoon TV. But what I wish is that someone else knew about me, Stacey, for instance, so I could turn to her and say, "Oh, the irony," in an ironic, dramatic voice, and we could laugh about it together. At least I've taken a seat in the back row and can sneak my book under the desk, ignore the molested loser, and secretly read. Therese's appeals are successful, and she enters Carmel at age fifteen. The reverend mother thinks she is spoiled, and the other nuns seem annoyed by her early entrance into Carmel, and by how she is babied by her real sisters, Marie and Pauline. Therese is torn between thinking the whole things sucks—though she claims to love humiliation because it pleases Jesus—and feeling joyous to be suffering for the Lord. When Therese becomes ill at the convent, she continues with the hard physical labor and long hours of prayer at Carmel. Therese writes, "How surprised you would all be if only you knew the martyrdom I have suffered this past year!"

Stacey chips off her nail polish with her pen lid while the woman talks about the time her uncle Don molested her in the alley behind the IGA. One time! Her Uncle! Boo-hoo. She is the color of skim milk, with a frizzy blonde perm, no wedding band, and a lumpy ass. Somewhere in the visitor's parking lot is a car with faded "I believe Anita" and "Keep Your Laws off My Body" bumper stickers.

I slip Stacey a note that says, "It was probably the only time this super-hag ever got any."

Stacey looks down, silently gagging in disgust and I smile at her so sweetly that she has to cover her mouth like she's coughing. She passes the note to Ashley Vallano, then points back at me. Ashley presses her lips together, swallows her laugh, and gets to work scribbling a cartoon. Then she gives it back to Stacey, who almost cracks up before she hands it to me. Ashley has drawn two stick figures lying next to a trash dumpster heaped with dented cans and cardboard boxes. One stick figure is crying out, "Give it to me, Uncle Don!"

The woman paces back and forth by the chalkboard, telling about her feelings of low self-esteem after "the incident," how her grades dropped, how she couldn't relate to her friends. Now she stands at the window, streaking one finger against the frosted glass.

"This could be happening to someone you know. If one of your friends seems withdrawn or sad, please, please, try to get her help. Or, Heaven forbid, if it is happening to you, please talk to one of the counselors here at Therese of Lisieux."

But the one counselor here, Sister Clare, devotes her time to watching The Price is Right on the black and white TV in her office and eating Rice Krispie treats. No one would be stupid enough to tell her their personal problems; she gets rattled when she can't find a pen. But let's say I snapped and told her, "Sister Clare, my father and I have been sexual partners for two years now. My parents experienced a 13 year period of infertility after my birth. The month my father started having intercourse with me was also the month my mother finally conceived. So, in a way, my father and I having sex is what allowed two other precious humans to be born. Sister Clare, may I have a Rice Krispie treat? Sister Clare, my father says most people don't have the intelligence to understand our union, and indeed it is a delicate situation. He believes that Society is filled with mundane, conventional thinkers who use only ten percent of their brain power. My father is using his whole brain; he has entered the Mind at Large, where one is free from societal restraints. Due to the stupidity of those who don't understand the Mind at Large, we must keep our relationship a secret. For a while I believed in his theory, but I have now transcended The Mind at Large, Sister Clare."

And then my problems would be solved. Sister Clare would call Social Services and my little brother and sister and I would be placed in foster care, where, according to newspaper stories, we would be cared for by "parents" on Crystal Meth, fed dry dog food and burned with cigarettes.

Now the bell rings and we each thank the valiant, molested hag before leaving the classroom. She grins modestly, believing she has made a difference.

In the hallway, I whisper, "Oh, Uncle Don!"

Ashley says, "Nobody gives me sweet lovin' like my man Uncle Don."

"Do me, Donnie," Stacey says. "For real, though, I mean that is tragic to be molested by your very own uncle."

Ashley nods, and I agree: oh yes, yes, what could be more terrible. But I'm disgusted she would fall for this loser lady's sob story. Stupid-ass Stacey and her perfect life.

Stacey grabs my wrist and brings it to her face, inhaling. "You smell awesome. What's that you're wearing?"

I buy Junior Mints from the vending machine and skip lunch hour to go to the library and read "The Story of a Soul." The library is officially closed over the noon hour, but the librarian, Sister Mary Elise, goes to the teacher's lounge with her sad little thermos of soup and leaves me the keys. I lock the doors behind her then curl up in the book nook, a quadrangle of cushy plaid couches in the back of the library by the windows. The couches were donated by the O'Fallons, a family with five luminous, slutty daughters, and it has been said that if you so much as sit on the couch you'll contract genital warts, that if the bare skin of your arm grazes the plaid material you'll get scabies, and that the many stains are not from spilled Cokes in the O'Fallon basement, but dried menstrual blood and sperm.

I stretch out on the couch, sink my head into the pillowed arm rest, and finish "The Story of a Soul." Then I re-read the sections I originally found ludicrous, because now I understand her whole story, now I see how wrong people are about Therese, how they try to present her as a pure, rose-scented princess who slaved to win hearts for Jesus, ignoring her "scruples," her pain, her vanity, her desire for glory, ignoring the simple fact that a girl like her could have problems. And I know why she wanted to escape from her father's house, but I will not share this with the class next week when I present my hagiography. The secret of the little flower is mine.

Therese found her freedom in death. I will not be forced to wait so long. One day my whole life will be like this moment; I will have a big loft apartment in New York City with many books and couches and a shiny ring of keys. Caroline and Xavier will live with me, and I will walk them to school each morning before I go to my college classes, and on my lunch break I will have mango juice and a chocolate croissant and I will wear tall leather boots and many, many men will love me from afar but I will shun them coldly.

Okay. Here is the other thing: Behold, I show you a mystery. My hands smell of flowers when I think of Saint Therese, like right now, a detectable sweetness is rising from my hands, filling the book nook with the smell of fresh, cold roses. This is not the sort of fact I can use in my hagiography; this cannot be from Sister Beth's tiny rose brushing my hands. Possibly Therese, in her new world, has considered my suffering and sought to console me. Possibly, following in the tradition of so many great saints, I am headed for the mental ward.

To calm myself I close my eyes and hold each Junior Mint on my tongue like a Eucharist wafer until it melts.

After school, I stop in at Stacey's again, just to taunt myself. Today her mother serves fudge brownies topped with cream cheese icing.

"Another, Kendra?" Mrs. Ramos asks. Her nails are painted a creamy ivory that fades into the swirls of pale icing as she carves another brownie out of the pan and puts it on my plate. Stacey touches her skirt where it grazes her stomach then jumps up and shrieks, "Jesus Christ, there's never anything to eat in this house that's not fattening."

Mrs. Ramos slams the brownie pan on the table. She flips open the refrigerator door and shouts in Spanish, pointing at a row of bright tangerines, cups of yogurt, a bag of baby carrots, and a bowl of chopped broccoli covered with plastic wrap. Stacey grabs a tangerine and starts to peel it, then sighs and takes another bite of the brownie. Then Stacey and her mother sputter out a few giggles before they both crack up. The daisies on the table are wilting and I concentrate on their limp petals while I laugh along with my best friend and her beautiful, attentive mother, ha, ha, ha, ha.

I walk home. The crystalline snow of yesterday has melted to dirty slush, and I must have been smoking crack to think Saint Therese was blooming from my palms, because I smell like nothing at all.

I suppose I am not meant to have a life like Stacey. Jesus has a plan for each of us—this is what I hear every day at school and it certainly makes Jesus sound like a big retard sorting through his accordion file: Jenna Kellerman should go crazy; I'll have Kelli Rohan hook up with a loser junkie who will devour her life; Stacey Ramos will know nothing but happiness.

Perhaps Jesus' plan for me is to suffer, and I should try to find some glory in it, as Therese did. "Saint Kendra" I whisper. Then to prove I am not going loony, and also to prove He holds no power over me, I say right out loud: "Fuck Jesus Motherfucking Christ," and frighten the paper boy who goes barreling past me on his bike, appalled.

Mom is asleep on the couch—she may be contending for a medal in the sleeping Olympics—and Xavier is crashed out in his playpen, sleeping like a tiny prisoner with his hand cupping a half-empty bottle of milk. Caroline is slumped in the baby swing, all her little chins folding, and she waves her hands and offers up a bird-like shriek. Mom sleeps on. I pick up Caroline and notice that she smells a bit ripe, so I carry her to the bathroom, lay a fat towel down in the tub and wash her carefully with Phisoderm and lukewarm water. The baby books say a three-month old is supposed to hate baths, but she's very jolly, splashing around with her balled fists. I lift her head gently to wash the frizz of curls at the back of her neck, then dry her off, put her in a clean diaper and sleeper and take her back to mom.

"Oh Kendra, you scrubbed up the little bug-a-boo," Mom says.

I hand Caroline to Mom, and lift Xavier out of his play-pen. He runs a few frantic laps around the living room before I wave my hands and swing my hips, coaxing him to dance. Then he shimmies with a look of earnestness that kills me.

"Kendra," Mom says, laughing, "you're such a genius with babies. You're such a big help to me. I don't know what I'd do without you."

I don't even look at her.

Across the street at Mrs. Blumenthal's house, purple and yellow crocus are pushing up through the snow.

I pick up Xavier and say, "Flowers, pretty flowers," and tap the glass.

I bundle up the dirty baby laundry and towels and plunge downstairs to start the wash before dinner. I pour a whole cup of detergent into the machine against the wishes of Dad, who always says this is the manufacturer's way of ripping off the consumer, hat only a half cup is needed.

Therese's sister, Marie, once told her that fidelity over small things is what matters most, and Therese never forgot this. The detergent swirls through the water, streaks of blue turning to white bubbles.

I've planned how to start saying no, decided how things are going to change, really change, and here we are at it again for the second night in a row. Probably I will get another urinary tract infection and need to sneak off to Planned Parenthood for antibiotics. I let myself sink into it, again and again, my hatred for my father softened by memories of his past kindness, his past innocence, a wreath of violets and white carnations he gave me on my First Communion, a photograph of him at 12 with bony shoulders and patched denim shorts that bleeds into the current vision of our naked bodies twisting on the bed, the condom's foil wrapper on my night stand: Hi, Dad; wishing he would choke me or run me over with his car and in the hospital all would praise me for my bravery and how clear it would be that I was abused and innocent, not like the murkiness of this moment where my back rounds up off the bed, where I realize my sole escape from this night, from the memory of all our nights, is the grave. I'm busy imagining my swan dive off the high, arcing roof of Therese of Lisieux, the glorious feeling of falling and falling and falling though the school is only three stories high, so at first I don't notice the smell of roses but soon it's powerful and pouring out of me, like I'm sweating out a garden, like plumes of red-pink smoke will rise off my hands, and I am a rose, my pulsing veins a tangled vine, my brain blossoming with calm joy, the stony bloom of my heart unfurling now—loved, not forgotten—and the angels and saints swirl around my bed, their eyelashes brushing my forehead as my father lifts his head, alarmed, as if he smells smoke.

"What that smell?" he asks, darting his head around.

Therese of Lisieux is known as the people's saint, for the people loved her so. In this second, I am just another amazed pilgrim, and I raise my hands up in the air as if I am lifting a body, my new body, and I offer Therese my first novena of gratitude.

"Oh, thanks," I whisper.

Now Dad jumps out of bed, tripping on the sheet. "Why are you thanking me? What's that smell?"

I shrug my shouders in the scented darkness. "It's me."

The Patron Saint of Girls

Girls, look up here! See me hovering close to the water-stained ceiling, above the humming VCR. Behold, I am Agnes, patron saint of girls, come to distract you from the climax of your freshman biology class, the video *How Christian Girls Blossom into Maturity*.

Perhaps they have not told you about me. At fourteen I martyred myself for the King of Kings, and thus lost my own chance to blossom into earthly maturity. In life, I was adored for my perfect, girlish beauty, but boys held no allure for me. My heart belonged to my heavenly husband, Jesus Christ. My suitors, furious that they couldn't sway me with their charms, revealed me to the Roman governor as a Christian girl who would not marry. The governor ordered me to choose an earthly husband, but I would not. He then remanded me to a house of prostitution, and gave all Roman citizens liberty to defile me, but Jesus protected my purity by rendering the Romans awe-struck in the face of my devotion. When the governor ordered me dragged from the house, my former suitors raised me above their heads, whispering, "Light as a feather, light as a feather," and I ascended from their fingertips and floated five feet above them.

The governor's servants had prepared a red-hot rack for me in the yard. I tumbled to the ground and, in the raw dreaminess of the moment, laughed and raced to grab the iron hooks that would pierce my hands. Seeing my willingness to accept the rack, the governor instead ordered me beheaded. On a spring green knoll dotted with buttercups and milkweed, an executioner began by hacking off my braids and flinging them to the weeping crowd. A group of my friends held hands and crooned softly, "Goodbye dear Agnes, our sweet friend. Heaven deserves you. We'll meet again."

I knelt on the tender grass and bowed my head, waiting in valiant bliss to meet Jesus. As the executioner raised his sword, I heard my best friend's voice rise above the chorus. "No!" Melissa shrieked. "Agnes, please stay!" I lifted my head and saw, through the crush of people, her sunny, freckled face buckle into tears. Then the executioner grabbed me by my newly-shorn hair and lopped off my head.

But why am I blabbering about myself when there will be a quiz tomorrow on *How Christian Girls Blossom into Maturity*? Look here: Sister Edith Clare O'Hagan, the narrator, says that a girl who respects herself will find a boy who respects the fact that she's a virgin. Sure she will. By the way, it's kind of you not to laugh at Sister Edith's ultra-suede pantsuit and her choppy, frizzed hair. Older nuns who started out in wimples and habits often bear an understandable grudge against the ever-changing world of civilian fashion. There is the odd exception—your history teacher, Sister Kathleen—

pure Grace Kelly with her chignon, stacked heels and patent leather handbags. I could have appeared to you in jeans and a T-shirt, or a mini skirt and Manolo Blahniks, but in the material world, your outward appearance can lend you credibility, so I've chosen my saintly attire: a chaplet of pearl roses to reign in my tumbling curls and offset my beatific face, a flowing ivory gown, soft leather sandals.

Now, Sister Edith says Christian girls should *never* have sex before marriage. Shocking. But I've been watching these films for decades now, and they truly are becoming more progressive. They used to rely on animated schools of fish swimming madly into a stone-lipped culvert wearing red lipstick. And their idea of straight talk about menstruation was "Don't wear light-colored clothing during your special time, and bathe daily." Really, you girls at Saint Therese's Academy are luckier than your predecessors.

I know you're thinking, *Oh, sure, what would old Sister Edith, sex machine, know about sex before—or after—marriage!* But Sister Edith did have sex in her youth, before she became a bride of Christ. Her lover, a sensitive young man (there are some—currently twenty-seven, I believe, in North America: consider it a scavenger hunt!) was unschooled in the ways of passion, and extremely nervous. Therefore, the sin-to-pleasure ratio was not favorable. Little wonder Sister Edith now says that Christian girls should follow the Jesuit example and enjoy the life of the mind: science, art, drama and literature, while all non-scholastic energies should be channeled into sports. Learn to spike a mean volleyball and win a college scholarship. Go to the YWCA and swim laps until you are famished. Get a gang together and go bowling! And guard against one-on-one situations with boys where desire could lead to depravity and pure foolishness. God is watching!

But the good news and the bad news is that God, as all-powerful as he is, cannot hold vigil over every girl at all times. For instance, you, in the back row, Jody Renneker, a responsible baby-sitter—you're feeling sick watching this video, because you and Brad Gryska stripped from the waist up and had a seriously freaky make-out session after you put the Clancy twins to bed on Saturday night. Oh, the searing guilt! But really, Jody, considering the hundreds of millions of girls worldwide who had unwedded sex on Saturday night—and given war, and suffering, and the general despair of billions—can you honestly believe that God had time or cause to observe that you went to second base with Brad?

Afterward, you kissed Brad goodbye in the Clancy's foyer, against a backdrop of gold and silver foil wallpaper, and came away with the taste of wintergreen Chapstick and a flake of skin on your tongue—yours or his? You danced it around the roof of your mouth as he snuck out the back door. Yes, I watched; I sighed. You swiped one of Mrs. Clancy's Winston Light's from a kitchen drawer and smoked and shivered on the glacial back porch while Brad, illuminated by the street lights, trudged through the diamond-bright layer of ice that had formed on top of the snow. Suddenly and impossibly, bells rang out in the distance, harmonizing with the crunching sound of Brad's boots and giving a voice to the skittish new joy inside you.

Yes, I offered my girlish neck to the sword to avoid this sort of entanglement. And now I part company with Sister Edith on the sex issue. What's wrong with engaging the life of the mind *and* the life of the body? Consider this: at age seventy-five, you will still be able to curl up on the couch with a book, but you won't be able to run an impulsive lap around the house in the fresh snow, barefoot, to see how it might feel to be a martyr. You won't be able to listen to your mother cooking dinner downstairs, the splatter of grease in a pan, while the boy you've snuck through your bedroom window finger-traces the states on your naked back, the eastern seaboard through the Gulf Coast.

Why, there's nothing wrong with the joy of young bodies. I used to tell girls that if they could find a seventeen-year-old with a vasectomy, have at it! And if you can't, I said, put on a hat and sunglasses and head to the pharmacy. Protection was my motto. Some girls had sex and considered it to be a marvelous, wholesome adventure. But others felt cheapened and lonely, and wept over the phone to their friends until gray morning filtered through their bedroom shades. Each whispered lamentation—*Please tell me I'm not a slut*—was a blow to my own exuberant spirit. I paced in their bedrooms all night, silently admonishing myself for giving general advice, instead of tailoring my sex-talks to the needs of each girl. With my human girlhood cut short by fervent devotion, was I trying to relive my lost youth through these girls? Who was I, anyway? A girl who knew the great spiritual love of Jesus Christ, a girl who martyred herself for sexual purity. An unvanquished saint.

And that was before the advent of AIDS and potent new strains of other STD's. Now, what advice do I have for you? I'm as baffled as anyone else. My stupidity fills me with self-loathing, and the only cure for that is to eat five spools of cotton candy and take a nap. Through the haze of celestial sleep I hear other saints bad-mouth me as they flutter past my open window.

"Girl saints," huffs Gabriel the archangel.

"Well, perhaps not *all* of us are so dreamy and unreliable," brags Joan of Arc, Miss-Hotshot-Peasant-Who-Saved-France.

But listen to you mean girls laugh as Sister Edith delivers tips on developing "meaningful friendships" with boys. Is this really something to aspire to? Well then, you're in luck, because I know how to make boys like you, and it has zip-o to do with sex. I see a couple of you who like other girls romantically starting to nod off. You may have to fight ignorance during your time on earth, but we in heaven are not boy-girl fanatics as they would have you believe.

But with a boy, the world is different. There's no need to be the good-natured softball pitcher that you are in real life. The secret is that boys love tragedy, so trot it out. The worst thing that's ever happened to you—don't be shy! If you've been lucky enough to escape tragedy thus far, just make something up. And if he discovers you are a liar, he'll only find you troubled and interesting. It's a win-win situation!

Hey, now, don't hate the messenger! Wendy Charbonneau, look at you glaring at me. I know your sister Cindy and her best friend, Gayla, were killed in a car accident driving home from the Weston Mall, where they spent their last hours trying on platform clogs, shoplifting a lipstick sample from the Chanel counter, and drinking Pineapple Julius.

Just before the speeding Mustang plowed into her car, Cindy lit a Benson and Hedges, set the cruise control and said, "My God, this is a wonderful cigarette. I don't know why I was smoking those crappy generic ones when you only save, like, fourteen cents a pack. Benson and Hedges rule! If I have twin sons, or daughters, for that matter, I'll honor them with the names Benson and Hedges."

"Good idea," Gayla said, lighting a cigarette of her own. "I'll name my son Viceroy. 'Come, young Viceroy, come and sit in the parlor with mummy. Do bring your brothers Winston and Chesterfield.'"

"And your baby sister, Eve," added Cindy with a laugh. And then the Mustang.

The policeman gave your parents Cindy's purse in a plastic bag. Your dad handed you the bag, saying, "You can have this Cindy . . . I mean—Jesus!—Wendy." Your mom hugged you weakly, as if she'd turned into a frail stranger, a bizarre, startled senior citizen on a day trip. Later, you fished the stolen lipstick out of Cindy's purse, examined the nicked case, and then rolled out the smudged, gummy column of Vamp, the eggplant black color popular in all the magazines. On the morning of Cindy's funeral, you made a pilgrimage to the Chanel counter and stared at the empty space among the bright bullets of lipstick. The Chanel saleswoman passed you over to help a woman who was looking for a tube of Vamp.

"There is no Vamp," the saleswoman snapped. "Vamp is on permanent back-order." She clicked her opalescent nails on the counter. "Even the sample has vanished."

You wanted to pull the precious, contraband Vamp from the zippered compartment of your backpack, hold it up to the saleswoman's creamy, flawless face and scream, "It's only *lipstick*!" But you wondered, for a heartbeat, if God had given Cindy a harsh punishment for stealing. You edged away from the Chanel counter with salt tears dripping into the corners of your mouth, and raced through the maze-like cosmetics department, where suddenly the customers had all turned into imbeciles, inquiring about retro lip gloss and youth-infusion serum.

The Vamp is now in the cleaned-out bottom drawer of your maple chest, along with Cindy's hair brush, her jar of Carmex, her Daisy razor, her Great Lash mascara, her half-used bar of Clearasil soap, her toothbrush, and a string of dental floss that you pulled from the lining of the bathroom wastebasket. You distinctly hear Vamp's chic black case roll around when you put your clean socks and underwear in the top drawer. You will never wear that hallowed lipstick down to a dark nub, never even try it on, you will keep it, always.

I know you are horrified, Wendy, by the notion of using your beloved sister's death to make yourself tragically attractive to some clueless boy; you would never submit to the traitorous indignity of it. But Cindy wants you to know that it's fine with her! In fact, it's great with her. She wants you to tell her story endlessly until the boy starts to miss her, too. She'll be watching. Heaven's an observatory from which we peer down on the high drama of your everyday lives. You are entertaining the angels, unawares.

But I see anger smoldering through your flinty smiles. You're thinking, *Oh, the wise, wonderful, patron saint of girls, where were you when I could have used your help?* Wendy, I know, is just about bursting to ask why I didn't intercede on the day of Cindy and Gayla's car accident. And Caroline Kelly is wondering where ethereal Agnes was when old uncle Frank stuck his hand down her pants at the family reunion.

And you, Stacey Ramos, think I must have been off running tra-la-la through a heavenly field of flowers when your cousin Julie slit her wrists clean open with a boning knife after being dumped by her boyfriend, Henry. Oh, Stacey, you have every right to hate me. I should have appeared to your cousin in the bathroom, as she sat naked on the cold edge of the pink bath tub, balancing the knife on a creamy sea shell soap and staring down at the interlocking sea horses in the ivory linoleum. I should have whispered, "Julie, you're going to die some day anyway, and earth is a real kick." I should have wrapped her in those cotton towels the colors of saltwater taffies and said, "Look, Henry's a seventeen-year old poseur. He uses the word *Kerouacian*. Trust me, sweetie, there'll be bigger fish to fry."

But please, girls, forgive me for my errant ways, my deadbeat saintliness. Take pity on me, for I cannot bear to gaze down upon the theater of life for very long: the snap-decision suicides, the crashing cars, the tumbling bridges, the flaming houses, the hospitals where weary humans have their hearts and brains gutted and undergo the torments of skin grafts and chemotherapy.

Why are souls so hearty, so defiantly everlasting, while physical bodies—bones and blood and disease-prone organs— are so very delicate? Life on earth is but a breath of eternity; why must it so often be spent in anguish? I ponder this question with other saints, but fly off the handle when they bring up the book of Genesis. "That forbidden fruit and original sin crap is old as the hills," I scream, and then I'm admonished for my immaturity, my inability to discourse in a respectful manner. I want to pose my questions to the Son of God, but haven't worked up the courage. *See Jesus RE: human delicacy* filters through all my thoughts, a haunted procrastination.

Yes, I have failed you, but understand that I am a low-ranking and rather temperamental saint. My earth years and good works were few; my title is mostly honorary. Though canonized for blind devotion to Our Lord Jesus Christ, I was not particularly holy; I martyred myself in a crazed moment of girlish passion. And my devotion was not even pure. I fostered romantic inclinations toward a boy, Johnny.

"Hello, Agnes," he said once, his ruggedly sonorous voice transforming my name from sturdy to breathtaking: I was Catarina, Magdelena, Maria Rosa. My brain shattered into kaleidoscopes of shimmering, bewildered neurons. On that spring day when I martyred myself on the knoll, I spotted Johnny in the crowd, and was glad to be wearing the dove-gray dress that made my eyes glow, though I suffered slightly for him to see me with my hair chopped off. As the executioner brought the sword to my neck, my heart sang for Jesus, but an unchristian thought crossed my mind: *Now Johnny will see how different I am from all the other girls.* I thought Johnny might gallantly offer to duel the executioner, or at least yowl in protest, but it was only Melissa who cried out for me.

Knowing the less honorable truth, you girls might look on me as a heavenly lightweight, but I *am* trying to mature into the kind of saint who would fill your hearts with love and protect you from all evil. What responsibility! I often wish I could give up my saintly status and loll around like a regular heavenly girl. Cindy, Gayla and Julie, for example, are spending this morning ice skating, and this afternoon they'll go to a matinee. While they sit in the cool, daytime darkness of the theater, eating buttered popcorn and Twizzlers, I'll be appearing to the fifth hour biology class at Mary, Star of the Sea in Naples, Florida. Not that I'm complaining. I enjoy the everlasting company of my earthly family and the friendship of exalted saints. But, in heaven, as it is on earth, the friends you love best are those from your girlhood. Melissa and I go out for cappuccino all the time.

Just now, Cindy, Gayla and Julie have taken off their ice skates. Perfect layers of Vamp coat their lips. They sit on a split-log bench, drinking mocha lattes and smoking. In heaven, everybody smokes. When you arrive, you go to your favorite earth house, which exists here, room for room. Your family is here, and God is everywhere: in your mother's arms wrapping you in a wild hug; in your grandmother padding across the living room in her lace up, soft-soled shoes. Your dad sorts through his scratched LPs, sold at a rummage sale after his death, but now returned to their rightful place in the Silvertone console. But your little brother isn't at the house, and you panic, remembering all those times you told him to go to hell. Your mom, who retains her earthly telepathic abilities, takes your hand and whispers that he's on his way.

"Oh, Jesus," you say to those who've died before you, "it was so goddamn hard without you." (Because you have made it to heaven, you can take liberties.)

Then joy triumphs, as you realize everyone will get to spend eternity together in the Kingdom of God. Still, there are things to get used to. On earth you used to worry about your weight, but now, when you step on the old bathroom scale, that creaking purveyor of doom, you weigh exactly zero pounds; you are truly a spirit. Freaky! But wait, there's more. Open the medicine cabinet and find the pill boxes and amber prescription bottles filled with mints and gum. In heaven, you will never, ever see anyone dear to you standing at the bathroom sink, gulping down pills. Imagine the beauty of a world without illness or death, a world without end, Amen.

Though you spend eternity with your family and friends, and should, theoretically, be jubilant at all times, you aren't, of course. You retain your human girlhood spirit, and so you sometimes lie in bed on snowy winter days, mysteriously sad, listening to the thunder and clutching at your pillows.

"Mom," you call down through the heat register, "Is that really thunder?"

"Yes," she yells up from the kitchen, "thunder-snow."

Thunder-snow. You whisper the word to yourself over and over in your darkened celestial bedroom. Because in heaven you are still *you;* you are not secretly transformed into a cease-lessly happy moron, like some contestant on *Bible Boys and Gospel Girls.*

But I see Sister Edith is bidding you farewell and the credits are rolling in all their cheap glory. So much for doing well on your quiz tomorrow. You girls must think I'm a real throw-back—Grandma Agnes!—to have wasted so much time talk-ing about boys, but I was gearing up to say that it's far more important to be kind to each other. Never forsake kindness for cleverness, and guard against the poison of vengeful thoughts. (I was never one to resist voo-doo dolls, but careful: the power of the human hex is abundant.) Sure, you want to win the Westinghouse Science Award or be class valedictorian, but don't rat on each other to gain favor with the teachers: in heaven, there are no ass-kissers.

And now you girls are off to lunch. Oh, I miss you al-ready. My days as a flesh and blood girl were too few. I'll be no more than a curious memory by the time three o'clock rolls around and you climb on the school bus, where you'll sit quietly reading the collected works of Edna Saint Vincent Millay, or sneak a cigarette, or be shot by a wandering psychopath, or have the Virgin Mary appear etched in the frost of your window. Heaven is constant, but life on earth is bewilderment, pure innocence, for who among you knows the future?

Well, enjoy your pork burgers, green beans almondine, tater tots and frosted brownies. Watch the girl next to you as she eats, the long muscles contracting in her arms as she brings the pork burger to her mouth, the fingers that flutter and snap as she tells a story: "So I told him—*snap!*—to get, like, seriously lost." Watch her pliable neck as she flips her head forward in a violent seizure of laughter, the ends of her hair sweeping through the brownie's frosting. Watch all of your friends laughing and talking. Their bodies, those glorious, fallible machines, are at their well-oiled and fleeting best: no brittle bones or clogged arteries, no failed kidneys, crow's-feet or fading eyesight. Fat or thin, stumpy or tall, take joy in your earthly bodies!

And remember: kindness is providence. One girl doesn't talk much at lunch, doesn't touch her food. Her green beans congeal; her burger cools. Her particular drama remains a mystery, but you recognize the mood. As she rises to return her lunch tray, grab her arm and yank her back down in her chair. Tell her it's ten whole minutes til lunch is over. Tell her she shouldn't have skipped Vocal Music—Sister Jean Ann explained how to sing out of your *diaphragm*. Point to the pack of Camels and the Hershey's kisses scattered in the cavity of your backpack. Explain your theory that a fifth major food group—nicotine and chocolate—is essential for the health and well-being of growing girls.

When she pleads, "The library—I have tons of studying to do," hold her hand in yours and say: "No! Please stay."

Glory to God in the highest, and peace to his people on earth. See ya.

Saint Martha

Saint Therese of Lisieux asked Jesus to make her suffering greater. Saint Rose of Lima scrubbed her gorgeous face with pepper and washed her hands with lye. Saint Agnes accepted the rack, then raised her head to the Roman swords. Saint Christina the Astonishing flew out of the coffin and observed her own funeral from the church rafters. I had nothing in common with these girls, all born after Christ's own days on Earth, for I lived during Christ's time. They prayed to Jesus Christ, but I did not. To me, he was a flesh and blood man. And I did not crave veneration; I did not embrace austerity. I did not aspire to perfection, though I sometimes sought it in others. I did not wish to be the symbolic wife of Christ, forced to share my spiritual husband with countless other women.

I wanted to be the physical bride of Christ. I wanted Jesus to gaze upon me, Martha, and shudder with tormented desire. I wanted the King of the Jews to dust the disciples and spend sunny afternoons with me, gathering daisies and wild blue veronica in the bright fields north of Bethany. I wanted to stare at the face of the messiah—my Jesus!—all day long. When Jesus spoke in public, I often couldn't see him through the crowd, so while I listened to his prophecy, I looked around at the people craning their necks to see the savior. Blinded with awe, they never noticed me staring at their astonished, jubilant faces. I knew that if Jesus did fall in love with me, if he married me, I might disappear. Joy could levitate a person, and with the love of Jesus, I might float away like a soft curl of cedar falling from the carpenter's knife, a chicken feather carried by the wind. And yet, how I hungered to be seen, to be part of the story: Mrs. Jesus Christ.

My desire was my flaw. The women who worked at Bethany's leper colony embodied the glorious, modest holiness that Jesus adored. They didn't crave admiration or make a grand show of their sanctity; certainly they never stained their lips with elderberry or lined their eyes with kohl. Their Goodness was real, untainted by the vanity which colored my own daydreams about working with the sick—how fine it would be to lift a cup of water to the mouth of a parched and grateful leper just as Jesus strolled by! I would be enshrined in a panel of sunlight, with my hair cascading down my back.

I believed Jesus Christ possessed enough goodness for both of us; he didn't particularly need a pristine, holy wife. A regular woman like myself would only highlight his perfection! My beloved sister Mary patiently endured countless theories about my romantic destiny. One early morning while we stood in the kitchen shaping the bread dough into flat loaves, the hazy dawn air and low clouds made me think of angels.

"Mary, this could be the day the angel of the Lord appears to me." I pressed my palm lightly to an oval of dough. "The angel will whisper, 'Martha, child of God, The Lord Jesus

Christ will soon propose marriage. Will you be his bride, will you someday be the queen of heaven?'"

Mary slapped the oven spade onto the table. "Don't you think his mother will be the queen of heaven?"

"Then I'll be the princess of heaven. I'll be seated next to Jesus on a golden chair, wearing a crown of dark red roses, when suddenly, through the sweet mist, I'll pick your face out of the crowd. I'll say 'Hark, there is my dear sister, come to join me in the kingdom of heaven.'"

Mary brought her hands to her heart. "And I'll say, 'Hark, who is that lunatic woman on the throne?'"

"Why do you think I feel so strongly about Jesus? And why did he befriend our brother? Could it be that God brought Lazarus and Jesus together so that Jesus might have an easier path to me? Hmmm?"

Together, we slid the loaves onto the spade.

"No," Mary said. "For that matter, Jesus might have an easier path to *me*."

"But you don't love him."

"Not like you," she agreed.

That night as Mary and I lazed outside the house, eating bread and oranges and counting the first stars, we saw our brother Lazarus running home. As he tore over the hill, my heartbeat matched the staccato pounding of his feet.

"Mary," Lazarus screamed. "Martha!" He tossed down his satchel and cartwheeled to us. "Jesus Christ is coming to dinner tomorrow night."

A shrill, terrified ecstasy seized me. "No," I whispered, clawing at my face.

My sister pulled my hands from my face and kissed my fingertips.

"Oh, Mary," I said, "do you think it's true?"

Lazarus shimmied like a goat, kicking his feet in all directions. "Martha," he said, "believe me, Jesus will be here tomorrow night."

But Mary knew what I meant. She cried out, "Oh my God, Martha, maybe it is true."

And so with joy whipping through my body, I raced through the yard with my arms windmilling at my sides. I wanted to burn off some happiness so I wouldn't float away before Jesus started to love me. I spotted a clutch of white wildflowers glowing in the darkness and I picked them wildly, ripping them to confetti, except for one perfect bloom I saved for Mary. I raised the flower over her head, then crumpled the snowy petals into her hair and kissed her on the mouth.

I'd dreamed of him for so long! As Jesus Christ walked into our kitchen, I stared at him with my mouth hanging open, dumb as a fish. Then I sobbed like a baby pushed from the womb, overcome by the brightness of the world. Lazarus seemed embarrassed by my freakishness, and the disciples looked put off as well, but what did I care? Jesus was smiling at me. The disciples were a group of men like any other, by turns aggressive, loud-mouthed, violent and stupid; they were nothing to me.

Jesus was smiling at me.

I felt Mary tensing at my side as Lazarus introduced us to Jesus. Jesus' gaze was pleasant and democratic, though—did I dream it?—when he shook our hands, I believe he held mine longer. His warm palm pressed to mine offered the briefest picture of shared romance, a flash of craving and bliss, and when he pulled his hand away, I felt anchored by a new heaviness. I ached. My tendons and bones were craggy rocks and brass bars soldered with lead. Because with Jesus standing in front of me, I sensed how lonely I would feel when he walked out the door. I put my hand out to him again, then yanked it back, slapping the vase of lilies off the kitchen table. My sister picked up the flowers, motioned for Jesus to sit in our favorite chair, then *she* sunk down to the kitchen floor, and, in a rather cheap and obvious display of devotion, kissed the hem of his robe.

Then there was the smell of burning meat and a flurry of introductions to the other disciples. I turned away from Jesus to collect myself, then sunk my trembling hands into the kitchen mitts and pulled a charred rack of lamb from the oven. But the legs, which I'd seasoned with salt, spearmint, and my own tears—Fuzzy had been my pet—looked delicious. Would Jesus reflect upon my sacrifice as he feasted on the lamb? The gourds were nearly roasted, so I rubbed them with oil then dusted them with nutmeg, hoping Jesus might gaze at their burnished skins and imagine me planting thin seeds in the dirt and nurturing the tender plants to fullness. I tossed a few peppercorns into the pot of fish stew and admired my lemon pie—what I hoped would be the glory of my meal—allowing myself a few seconds to daydream about Jesus holding the delicate, lacy crust on his tongue.

How bizarre it was to prepare a meal with Jesus Christ looming in my peripheral vision. Conscious of my every movement, I strove for perfection and grace, and grew rattled. Where were the extra bowls I'd borrowed from the neighbors? I put the pie in the oven to brown and burned my fingers. My perfect curls frizzed from the humidity and sweat soaked my dress. So much food! Cooking for fifteen! I sucked on my fingers and motioned for Mary to help me, but she kept lollygagging at the feet of Jesus. "Tell me more," she crooned.

"Mary," I said, spilling the box of nutmeg on my dress. I tried to uncork the wine, but my burned fingers stung as I clasped the bottle.

"Mary! Please! Come help me!"

"In a minute," Mary said sweetly. She looked peaceful enough in an indigo blue dress that clung to her buxom figure.

"Mary," I hissed but she had fallen into rapture; she looked up at me groggily, as if I were a figure from a dream. The disciples turned to me, but Jesus kept speaking softly to Mary.

"Umm," I said, "Jesus?"

He turned away from my sister and smiled at me. The burning in my fingers stopped.

"Jesus," I said again, hearing the beauty of the name, the joy it would be to say over and over again: Jesus, is it raining?

Jesus, will you listen to me? Jesus, can you see my hands in the darkness?

The fish stew bubbled over the side of the iron pot and hissed into the fire, the sound of angels gasping at his magnificent smile.

"Oh, Jesus," I said. Everyone at the table waited for me to say the next thing. I didn't care about the dinner just then, because my head rang with wild, tuneless songs of devotion and desire, a lonely chorus I wanted him to hear.

"Yes, Martha," he said, clasping his hands together gently.

"I think my sister is in a trance, Jesus. Will you please tell Mary to help me?"

Jesus shook his head. "Martha, don't bother your sister. Can't you see that Mary and I are having a conversation? She has chosen to nourish the soul, not the body," he said, pointing at the platters of food. "Mary honors me greatly. You, in turn, should do the same. Do you understand nothing about my teachings?"

My mouth dried out, and so my top lip hung on one of my molars as I grinned a nervous dog-smile. As soon as Jesus left I would drown myself in the ocean and that would be that. Mary winced and mouthed the words, "I'm sorry." The other disciples combed the floor with their eyes, as if searching for some lost, treasured object. I, Martha-the-dog-girl, kept right on smiling. But the apostle Judas looked right at me, then pointed at Jesus and rolled his eyes.

Judas said, "Dinner smells delicious. Let's eat!"

*　*　*

The next morning, I woke craving death. For months I'd woken happy, refreshed from dreams of my life with Jesus, but now, with the sting of his rebuke, I felt in limbo, floating between despair and despair. I crawled out of bed and dressed, though I didn't bother to brush my hair or wash my face—what was the point? Mary had stayed up late, cleaning the kitchen after the disastrous dinner, so she was still sleeping. Lazarus had flitted off with the disciples. I lacked the courage to drown myself, so I walked out to the tangled grove of orange trees behind the house and flung myself down in the shade and cried. But the breezy darkness beneath the canopy of leaves soothed me, and I decided to live out there, beyond the house that forever would be tainted with Jesus' words. Martha of the Grove. My diet would consist of oranges, leaves, tender twigs and dirt. I licked the ground and discovered a bitter, floury taste, not unpleasant. Just as I took a full bite of earth, I heard my name called softly, from overhead. It was the disciple Judas.

"Martha," he said softly, "are you eating dirt?"

I ignored that question. Struggling to swallow, I curled myself into a sitting position.

He raised his brows and pointed to the ground next to me. I nodded, warily. Judas was just another reminder of my humiliation.

"Sure is a hot one today," Judas said, wiping sweat from his forehead dramatically. "Some soft rain would feel pretty good."

"Yes," I sighed, "that's true."

Somewhere else, the world glimmered with miracles.

"What brings me by," Judas said, clearing his throat, "is that I don't think I properly thanked you for the delicious meal."

"You're welcome," I snorted. But then a dozen scenarios of Jesus regretting his words whipped through my mind. I grabbed Judas by the shoulders. "Did Jesus send you? Did he?"

"No," Judas said. "I came on my own."

I let go of his arm and opened my eyes widely so I wouldn't cry. I concentrated on the waxy veins in the fallen leaves.

"Awfully sorry to disappoint you," he huffed.

"Well, I'm hardly a stranger to disappointment."

Judas sighed. "Jesus shouldn't have criticized you last night. I wish I'd said : 'Hey, Jesus, why don't you perform your miracle meal trick so Martha could just sit down with the rest of us?' Do you ever think of the right thing to say after the moment has passed?"

"Very often." I studied his face, warming to him. "But Jesus is changing our world with his miracles. Just having him in my house was a miracle."

"He is a good and brilliant man. And very popular with the ladies."

"What does that mean?" I snapped.

"The ladies love him. Of course, he's not supposed to love an individual, he's a gift to the world. You know that, right?"

"Of course."

"Why do you love him, Martha? Is it because he's in danger, because young Herod wants him dead, just like old King Herod did? The righteous outlaw seems to be a powerful aphrodisiac for women."

"Spare me from your filth, Judas" I said, and yawned luxuriously, though my face flamed with this new embarrassment.

Judas wiped a streak of mud from my cheek then stood and picked a runty, bruised orange from a low branch.

"No, take a better one," I said.

"The best fruit is saved for Jesus, right?"

Judas winked at me before he turned away. But his rogue charm caused me no suffering, for I still loved my Jesus.

Back at the house, Mary offered me a bouquet of bachelor's buttons and a chocolate bar. I wasn't quite ready to forgive my sister for her role in my dinner party humiliation, so I shunned her the entire day. But when I woke the next morning, stretching my hands over my head, I heard the softest clattering. Mary had crafted a bracelet of dark seashells and slipped it over my wrist as I slept. She stood at the window watching me admire the bracelet, and when I looked up at her bloodshot eyes and her soft, repentant expression, I shot out of bed and wrapped her in my arms. I though of Jesus, too busy being the messiah to spend time with his family. He claimed oceans of admirers, and twelve disciples, but with the exception of Judas, they never questioned his actions, so he didn't enjoy an equal relationship with any human being. I suspected he was often lonely—ha, ha, Jesus!—while I always, always had the comfort of my sister, and this evil thought cheered me immensely.

Our brother Lazarus came home ill, jolting me from my indulgent mourning. Mary and I sent him to bed and brought him cups of water. He would not take any food.

"See how drawn he looks," Mary said.

I covered him with a blanket because I couldn't bear to watch his bony, scabbed chest rise with each breath.

"Jesus should have sent him home earlier," I hissed. Lazarus had been trailing after those that trailed Jesus: a sort of second-rate disciple.

Lazarus opened his eyes, and whispered, "Don't be so critical, Martha. *I* wanted to stay with him. It was Jesus who begged me to go home and let my sisters care for me. And why didn't you put a lemon wedge in my water?"

That cheered us; illness hadn't dimmed our brother's bossy demeanor, so perhaps he was on the mend. But the days stretched past, and Lazarus weakened. Mary and I prayed fervently for him to recover, but my prayers grew bitter, prefixed with criticism: "Though possibly you haven't been listening, God," or "Maybe if you're not too busy, you could send your miracle-wielding son." I'd sent word of Lazarus' sickness to Jesus, and each day that he didn't appear, I grew more furious and despondent.

Where was Jesus! Lazarus' skin dried to a lizardy ash and when I rubbed salve on his papery lips, he cried silently. My previous, romantic view of illness, associated with strangers, injured birds, and the lepers—oh, the doomed lepers!—was moronic and shameful. There was no beauty in suffering.

"Dear God," Mary whispered, easing a fresh bandage over the rash that pocked his neck. Even Lazarus' thin snoring sounded wounded. "I can't bear it. First Daddy and then Mama, and now Lazarus." Without looking at me she said, "Don't let him die, Martha."

But he died the next morning.

Our parents died before the world spun with awe and testimony and miracles. Their death shocked us, and we wondered if we could survive the hurt. But the death of Lazarus was a betrayal. Because Jesus *could* conjure any miracle, we believed he had cruelly and inexplicably cheated us out of our brother. And so Jesus received a cool reception when he finally walked down the hill to our house with the other disciples streaming behind him in a weary funeral march.

"Martha and Mary," Jesus said, "I have come to see about Lazarus."

"Lazarus is dead," I said sharply.

"But if you had come earlier, Lazarus would not be dead, now would he? You should have saved him," Mary said, "Lazarus was your friend."

How proud I was of Mary's sudden boldness. I looked at Jesus and remembered happy afternoons strolling through the fields with my sister, weaving dandelion chains and daydreaming about meeting him—the messiah! My dream fiancee! Oh, the most divine bridegroom! Now, seeing Jesus, I shook with rage and fatigue. Exhausted by the galloping days, I wanted time to backtrack at the same speed: I wanted Lazarus back; I wanted my parents back; I wanted Mary and I to be children again, no, I wanted us to be not even born yet, I wanted my young father to leave a bouquet of rosemary at the house of my mother's parents, for my mother to kiss each fragrant leaf in the dark before hiding them under her pillow.

But then Jesus wept. He held his face in his hands, and fell to his knees. He looked at Mary, and then back at me. "Do you believe I am the savior? Do you believe I am the messiah?"

We said yes. We were mostly humoring him.

Sobs cut his voice as he screamed, "Take me to Lazarus."

And then we were off, flying through the fields of Bethany, the weeds crackling at our ankles like brush fire. Mary and I beat Jesus and the disciples to the tomb because we were country girls and good runners, or maybe just because their feet were sore from traveling. The two of us grabbed hands, and stood silently, panting, waiting.

"Lazarus," Jesus shouted, "come out of the tomb."

The silence was agony.

"Oh Lazarus, rise up," Jesus pleaded.

Mary gripped my hand tighter as Jesus went to enter the tomb.

"No," Mary called after him, "there will be a stench."

I thought of my brother's skin rotting, and saw the clouds swing down to my face as my knees buckled. I didn't tumble to the ground, because Judas watched my back, and he caught me.

"Thanks," I said.

Judas touched my arm, "Martha—"

I never heard what he said. Jesus ran out of the tomb, hugging himself and laughing. He raced past the disciples and pulled Mary and me into a quick embrace before he sprinted into the field with his hands raised over his head, a victory lap.

Next came Lazarus. He walked out of the tomb stiffly, pulling the burial bands from his wrists and then from his head, revealing his glowing skin and bright eyes. The disciples gasped. Mary pulled my index finger into her mouth and bit down hard, and we screamed because this was our life, not a shared episode from a dream that would leave us bereft when morning came. We tried to tackle Lazarus with kisses, but he zoomed past us—Lazarus was running!—crashing through the field, to Jesus. My brother and the messiah grabbed hands and dazzled us with a limb-flapping jig, their faces contorted with shock and joy. Watching them I wanted to live forever and knew it was possible—it was!—and yet I wanted to live not a second longer, for what could match seeing your brother rise from the dead, what could match this rough ecstasy that wore my throat raw from screaming, that chipped my bottom teeth in a fracas of hugs with Mary and the disciples?

We held an all-day party to celebrate. Everyone pitched in to prepare the noon meal and afterwards we relaxed with more red wine. Jesus kicked off his sandals, and I saw his cracked, hairy toes, jutting bunions and an in-grown toenail oozing greenish puss. He was too busy—he was letting himself go. Mary studied his feet, then unearthed the alabaster jar of nard oil and carried it into the kitchen. Our father had buried the jar in rocky dirt beyond the grove so his children would have something to sell if they fell upon hard times. Grinning slyly, Mary knelt and pooled the nard oil in her hands, then rubbed the messiah's feet. The other disciples nodded their approval, but Judas clanked his wine glass down on the table, and cried, "Mary, what are you thinking? You could sell that nard oil and feed the poor. You could fill the stomach of all the hungry babies in Bethany."

Mary's face hollowed and paled. Because despite the loveliness of her gesture, Judas spoke the truth.

Jesus started to pull his feet away, but then he looked at Mary's trembling mouth and reconsidered.

"The poor you will always have with you, but you will not always have me." Then Jesus blushed at his haughty words. "Leave Mary alone," he said, grimacing at Judas. "She's just trying to be nice."

Mary resumed her foot rubbing, zealously pouring too much nard oil on Jesus' toes. She blotted the excess with her hair, and the disciples cooed at her adoration—wiping the feet of the Lord!—but I knew see she wanted to condition her own curls, for nard oil bonds split-ends and makes your hair gleam like a child's.

Jesus looked at me, and, embarrassed to be caught staring at his bare feet, I turned my head and hummed a nonsense tune.

"Martha," Jesus said, "I'm sorry about that ridiculous comment I made when you were cooking dinner last time I visited. I was being oafish."

Jesus Christ: he was apologizing to me. The disciples frowned at this break in protocol. I shrugged my shoulders.

"Hmm. I 'm sorry. I don't remember what you're talking about."

Jesus smiled. "You don't remember my dinner party faux pas?"

I grinned back at him. His left eyelid drooped from the weight of a sty, and a spray of pimples reddened his chin. Swelled by rheumatism, his hands looked huge and boneless. As Mary lifted his foot and massaged his Achilles tendon, he closed his eyes and sighed. He seemed not at all like the son of God changing our lives with his miracles, more like a regular man enjoying a foot massage. A person. After the resurrection of Lazarus, I thought I'd risen above my selfish desire, but I ached with the urge to bend down close to Jesus and massage his temples with the gentlest pressure, before lifting his hair and kissing the soft cave of his neck. I knew men liked this, and I figured Jesus would, too. God, how I loved him! And if God had sent his son to earth in the form of a person, didn't he deserve to be loved as one? He was a thousand times more beautiful than any other man, and his gentle humility made him radiant. Jesus licked his cracked lips and I could taste the salt on my tongue.

Burning with shame, I slipped away unnoticed and sat outside the house. I raised my face to the afternoon sun, praying the heat would sear away my longing.

After a time, Mary came outside. As she crouched beside me, resting her small hand on my knee, I jerked away from her.

"Your hair looks lovely," I snapped, rubbing at the oiled hand print on my dress. "Very shiny."

"Martha," she said, "you need to get over it."

"How about you, foot-rubber?" But she was right. Jesus seemed to have the desired effect on my sister. She wanted to sing his praises and spread the word of his Goodness. I envied her simple devotion, for I coveted Jesus. Certainly I had no desire to share him with the world.

"Martha, I think you love the idea of Jesus," Mary said, "not the person."

"You couldn't be more wrong," I shouted. "Everyone else loves the idea of our Big Great Savior, but I love him as a person." My voice cracked. " I love him."

"You're not supposed to love him like *that*," Mary said.

I sighed. "I know. Believe me, I'm trying to harden myself to his beauty."

"Though you really wish he would harden himself to *your* beauty." Mary said solemnly. She made an obscene gesture with her hands.

"You, are, horrible," I said, weighting each syllable with disgust.

She kept motioning with her hands, and then startled me with a soft, excited noise, much like the call of a hooting owl. As I burst out laughing, Mary clapped her hands together triumphantly. We laughed until our stomachs felt tight and injured; we held each other drunkenly, and when it seemed like our laughter verged on dying out, Mary sputtered out the hooting owl noise and started us back up again.

Jesus smiled quizzically as he walked out of the house with Lazarus and the disciples.

"What's so funny?" he asked.

"Nothing," we said in unison, swallowing our laughter. Then the idea of telling him what was so funny struck us both at the same time, and we started laughing again. The men stood silently as we staggered hysterically around the yard. Jesus smiled like he was in on the joke, but it had little to do with him just then—it was a moment for Mary and me that existed apart from our divergent, perpetual adorations. Then, weary from laughing, my sister sunk to the ground and wiped away her tears. But the spell of merriment held me; I simply could not stop. My happiness was a new power, a magnetic sun that drew Jesus to me, and warmed him. As he touched my hand, I laughed out my love for him, for his acts that were so preposterously miraculous, it made you laugh, it did, and Jesus stepped closer, laughing with me, and I loved him, but I was still not content to be a faithful servant, I wanted him to love me above all others—to lovemelovemeloveme—and that was funny too, and the resurrection of my brother seemed hilarious—So, Lazarus, how've you been?—and Jesus knew every thought in my head; the owl joke had been spiritually transmitted. Jesus tossed his head back—a sensual, equestrian gesture that weakened me— and he laughed louder, and he came closer to me, closer still, and as I held out my arms to Jesus, he stole a quick glance back at the disciples. Their disapproving looks made us sick with laughter, because who were they to judge the son of God, and Mary's eyes were so wide, and pouting Judas crossed his arms over his chest, and my brother simply looked happy to be alive. And then Jesus stepped into my arms, and there he was embracing me when he should have been off curing the sick— Jesus the layabout!—and his hands touched my back, and I felt the patterns of his fingertips through my dress. Were you watching, Mary? I pressed my face to his neck and felt the pulsing of a small vein, and I kissed that vein, and our laughter died out as Jesus pulled me closer. A low, tremulous moan started in his throat as I raised my face and kissed his mouth.

My feet left the ground. I floated upwards a few inches until I was eye to eye with Jesus and we kissed again, the sudden feeling of fullness and lightness, as if my body had been stuffed with clouds. As I opened my mouth to his kiss, Jesus clamped his hands on my shoulders and shoved me back down to the ground.

He said my name gently, then scrubbed his mouth with his fist.

He turned and walked past the disciples, his robes snapping at his feet. The disciples shuffled behind him, staring at the ground. Mary and Lazarus stood silently, watching me with their mouths hanging open.

I never saw Jesus again.

But Judas came to me the following night, hovering beneath my window, his sick-bird voice rasping out my name. Electrified by Jesus' visit, I rose easily from bed. Indeed, I had not slept for two days. Whenever I closed my eyes, I felt Jesus' hands on my skin.

Careful not to wake Mary or Lazarus, I tiptoed through the house. Outside the moon flooded the earth with silver light, and I gasped at the sight of Judas. Blood caked his face. He held his cut and mashed hand tenderly in front of him, like a gift.

"Oh, Judas, what happened?" I wiped his tears with the cuff of my robe.

"Martha," he moaned, "I have to tell you something before I take my life. You have to know that it's not like they say. I'm not a traitor." He kissed me on the forehead, then turned away stiffly and vomited in the cold grass.

"Don't talk like that." I put my hand on his back. "Of course you're not a traitor, Judas. Everyone knows you're a good man. Come on inside and Mary and I will help you get—"

"No!" he screamed. He wiped his mouth with the back of his hand. "No, it's not going to be like that at all. I have something terrible to tell you."

"Judas!" I said, "You're scaring me."

"Jesus is dead," he said.

He clapped his hurt hands to my face to muffle my screams. But I was silent.

"Jesus is dead and the Pharisees planted a bag of silver coins on me to make it look like I revealed him as the messiah, to make it look like an inside job. Jesus is dead, and I'm suspected because I criticized him."

His insanity calmed me. I struggled from his hands.

"No, Jesus can't be dead, Judas." I spoke to him slowly, as if he were a child. "A bag of silver coins? What kind of idiotic detail is that?"

A snake coiled beneath a flat rock lifted it's metallic head and hissed.

"But, Judas," I whispered, "why are you bleeding?"

He placed a finger to his swollen lips. "Listen," he said, "the serpent carries my name."

The snake hissed again, and I jolted back, but Judas leaned close enough to kiss its flickering tongue and cooed, "Judas Hissscariot, Judas Hissscariot"

Just when I was sure the snake would strike Judas, he jumped away and undulated his body, an awful dance that flung drops of blood from his wounds.

"Judas Hissscariot." He hugged himself, preening like a madman.

I lost my confidence. Mary was a great one for politics, always reciting and analyzing the news of the day, but I never believed Jesus to be in danger. Just for a second, I allowed myself to wonder if he really could be dead. Jesus taught us that belief could save a person, so in turn, thinking he might be dead would help kill him. But the more I tried to push the thought from my mind, the more brightly it blazed: Jesus, lonely and frightened, Jesus' head gashed by a rock, Jesus impaled by a sword. I closed my eyes and forced a smile. I tried to meditate on fields of pale spring flowers: snowdrops, creamy yellow crocus, pink hyacinth. But Jesus blossomed in my mind—a dark red flower, foreign and beautiful, that wilted into a pool of blood.

My sobs pulled Judas from his dementia, and he tried to steer me back inside, but to step one foot in the house would be to acknowledge that Jesus was dead. Morning would come, and I would have to tell Mary. If I stayed outside under the bright moon, Jesus could always be alive for me.

Judas kissed my forehead. "There's no life for me now. They all believe I betrayed Jesus."

"Let's go, Judas," I cried. He took my hand and we walked off in the darkness together.

And Judas mistook that for love. Forever he was grateful for my love that saved him, and I would love him, but that would come later. Judas had been beaten badly, and so we walked slowly, though I wanted to run fast and hard, to feel the wind burn my lungs.

It was the first of many nights spent traveling to the safe anonymity of Egypt. How I missed my sister! I felt sick with sin; I could not have imagined that, centuries later, Mary and I would be chosen as saints. Me, the patron saint of cooks, hospital dieticians and servants? Hah! Our canonization was a mystery. Neither of us claimed a single glorious deed. My sister's temperament was lovely, saintly perhaps. I was a regular girl, maybe worse. Each night of that journey, I thought of abandoning Judas, of leaving him scrabbling along in darkness while I raced back to Bethany. But I stayed with him. We distracted ourselves from the death of Jesus with our adventure.

We did not find out about the resurrection and ascension for some time.

On the dustiest days in Egypt, I would beg God to let a drop of rainwater fall from the sky, a signal that Mary still daydreamed of me. Sometimes I saw a bead glistening on my old seashell bracelet, or felt a drop graze my nose, and whether that was silliness or sweat and longing or divine intervention, it comforted me.

But I made a life for myself, like anyone does, and Judas and I were happy in Egypt. God blessed us with two children, Sarah and Ezra, whom we raised with guarded joy. We did not raise them as Christians, because to be a Christian—to follow Jesus—was to perpetually hunger for your own miracle, waiting for thrills, redemption, the bright promise. There was marvel and beauty in the waiting, but I never wanted my children to be that hungry. Jesus Christ was the folly of my vain girlhood, and as a woman, I had no use for him. But on hot summer nights when Judas' snoring kept me awake, I would wander the house, putting cold cloths on my children's faces, then stand at the window drinking a cup of water. I sometimes found myself at the door frame, looking up at a starless sky. I had the foolish and powerful feeling that I was the only person awake in the universe and I thought: I tried so hard. Why didn't you love me?

Saint Catherine Laboure

A monarch butterfly. Skull and crossbones. An exploding heart. Red roses. Wylie Coyote. Zoe's Exotic Skin Art and Piercing is wallpapered with beautiful possibilities. Welcome. Sprite or Coffee? Take a look inside the binder on the coffee table, where you'll find photographs of piercings: eyebrow, tongue, nipple, clitoral hood, and the famed Prince Albert, worth taking a peek at if you've never been with a well-pierced man.

But you're shaking your head. You have no interest in punching another hole in your body; you'll stick with your pierced ears and nose. How sad you look! Despondent, really. All this gray and rain. Yes, I think a tattoo would cheer you up. You're clutching a rumpled picture of the yin yang sign, big as a silver dollar, which you'd like tattooed on your lower back. Perfect! Follow me to the back room, my inner sanctum. Sit here on the padded table, which is swathed in hygienic paper. Yes, it is rather like a gynecologist's office, but I think you'll find getting a tattoo more pleasurable than a pap smear. And I am an immaculate worker—there is zero risk of infection. Look at the Comet-scrubbed counters and sink! I use only disposable needles and ink caps, and my tattoo gun is fresh from the autoclave, where devilish heat renders all instruments sterile.

Relax. Take off your shirt, leave on your bra.

You're having second thoughts about the yin yang sign? Instead you might honor your favorite band by tattooing the Seven Year Bitch logo on your ankle? I'm not so into these new bands; I'm a Stevie Wonder woman myself. I'll have to take your word that Seven Year Bitch is the bomb. But cruelly, the road from *au courant* to corny is unpredictable. Imagine a middle-aged lady like me with the Rolling Stones tongue licking her veiny ankle or the "Keep on Truckin" sign tattooed on her ass.

Forgive me. I see this last image troubles you.

Let me suggest another possibility, for in truth, I am more than a skin artist. I am Saint Catherine Laboure, and the glorious miraculous medallion is my trademark design. Clearly, though, I have revealed myself too soon, because I see the smirk beyond your smile, the phrase forming in your mind: Oh holy shit, it's Our Lady of the Tattoo Parlor.

But wait, look at the yin yang sign in your hand. Watch it lose its black and white symmetry as it transforms into your mother's senior yearbook picture. She is one year younger than you are now and seized by teenage lushness: her hair flows in perfect, glossy waves, her skin is a dream. You've admired your mother's angora sweater, but you've never noticed her necklace, a thin chain anchoring a small silver medallion. Look closely: carved in the medallion is a picture of the Virgin Mary arced by the words, *O Blessed Mother, protect us!* On the flip side of the medallion, a delicate M intertwines a cross, and there are two hearts, one crowned, and one pierced with a sword. Stars float in the background. This is a miraculous medallion, conceived by none other than the Blessed Virgin Mother herself. Your own mother wore her medallion religiously until the winter morning she flung it into the frigid waters of Lake Okaboji.

Your hands tremble. I didn't mean to startle you with my saintly animation. I sought you out because your sorrow has been mine. Your mother died two years ago today of a heart attack—a death for old men who enjoy fatty pork sandwiches and Lucky Strikes, not a thirty four year old vegetarian. You sit in lecture halls and wonder, again and again, until the wondering becomes its own yearning language—why would God allow your mother to die? She was your whole family. Your father is merely a check that comes once a month, a distant figure in the background of your childhood snapshots. You imagined that at college you would metamorphasize into a whole new creature: clever, attractive, mysterious and happy. But in this new place, your sorrow is fresh. Your mother has died all over again.

This morning you skipped class and strolled downtown, fixing your pained, gentle gaze at the shop windows. You stared through the frosted glass at Ray's Guns and Ammo, watching a man in an orange hunting vest point a rifle at the deer head mounted above the cash register. You stopped at the Love Garden and flipped through the used CD's wearily. At Sugartown Traders you tugged on a vintage cocktail dress, though all your joints mysteriously ached. The dress was too small. At Paradise cafe, you sat at the bar, and popped a few Dexatrim before ordering a double espresso and turtle cheesecake. And then you walked next door, to Zoe's Exotic Skin Arts, and found me waiting.

I hope my knowledge doesn't frighten you. And I'm sorry I convinced you to take off your shirt and then startled you. In retrospect it seems like a boy's cruel trick. Now, while I snap on my rubber gloves, let me assure you that this is not a mere alien encounter. You are, in fact, having an authentic religious visitation. And to think you laughed at news reports of that lady in Oregon who claimed her stone statue of the Virgin wept salty tears and blood. Certainly you are not being tapped for sainthood, nor am I about to relay a cryptic message from the Lord. I'm only here to influence your choice of a tattoo, my contribution to the story of your body. While a dermatologist can blast away the tattoo, this procedure is painful, and has uncertain results, for what is seared into the skin is always remembered.

Seared. That's just a figure of speech. A tattoo is a mere ink injection. And your tattoo will be as beautiful as the event that inspired it, which is my own story.

I was born in France in 1806 and baptized as Zoe Laboure. I enjoyed a happy infancy and early childhood until I was eight years old, and my mother died. My father did not understand the hard sorrows of a child, and so my consolation during this time was my beloved sister Louisa. But two years after my mother died, Louisa left home to join the Sisters of Charity of Saint Vincent de Paul. And then my life spiraled into perpetual housework and despair. It was cooking meals for my father and the two of us eating in silence; it was me at the kitchen window, drinking cold tea and praying for my sister to return. And so I dreamed of joining the Sisters of Charity, not because a passion for Jesus flamed in my heart, or because I felt particularly suited to the vocation. I simply missed my sister and imagined a blissful reunion, the hours we would spend sharing childhood reminiscences: A simple game called hide the boot that sent us into hysterics, the triumphant day our skinny tom cat wandered back home, waking on Saint Valentine's day to find our bed covered with pale pink hearts our mother had cut from tissue paper and sprinkled with confectioner's sugar.

My father raised much opposition to me joining Louisa, for with me gone, who would care for him? Finally, at the great age of 24, with his grudging permission, I joined the Sisters.

My first morning at Saint Vincent de Paul, the Reverend Mother granted my sister and me a rare private visit in the garden. I flung myself onto Louisa and held her for one glorious second. After all our years apart, there we were: the Labouré girls, shrouded from the world by a heaven of buttercups, blue hydrangea and sprays of wild lavender. But Louisa broke the spell with a dry kiss to my cheek. She pulled my hands from her waist.

"I shall love you no more than my other sisters of Saint Vincent de Paul," Louisa announced.

"But Louisa," I said, "we really *are* sisters."

Her girlhood beauty was gone. A wrinkle gripped the skin between her eyebrows like a hawk's claw.

"Poor, poor Zoe," she whispered imperiously, "you have much to learn."

She was right. I had not prepared myself for the rigors of the convent: the incessant structure of prayers and physical labor, the lack of sleep, the enforced silences. Life at home seemed easy compared with this new austerity. But I struggled through my postulancy, and was given the name Catherine. Ballooned by the starchy food and wearing an ivory muslin gown and a crown of rosebuds, I marched myself down the chapel aisle and married that silent, far-off bridegroom, Jesus Christ. And then the sisters—my sisters—packed the dress away for the next girl, and shaved my head.

That night, as I shivered beneath my blanket, I heard another sister singing. At Saint Vincent de Paul, we slept dorm-style, 10 cots lined up on either side of the room. In the darkness, I couldn't tell who was singing, or if anyone else was awake to hear the Ave Maria, heaven's best siren song. Though her voice was deepened by an obvious chest cold, and muffled by a pillow, the beauty of the sister's song pulled me out of my bed: *Ave Maria, gratia plena, dominus tecum.* I stood on the cold floor, wanting to dive into the Ave Maria over and over, until my body released my soul like a winter bird flying past the dark night. When her singing stopped, I walked out of the cold room, though it was forbidden, and went to our chapel to pray.

I flung myself in front of the altar.

"Jesus, Son of God," I whispered, " Oh, let me join my mother in heaven."

The smell of warm peppermint made me lift my head. A column of pink light funneled down upon the statue of the Virgin Mary to the left of the altar. A translucent white band, delicate as spun sugar, ribbonned the space where the light shone from the ceiling. And then she appeared, wearing the same drab gray robe as all of us sisters at Saint Vincent de Paul. I do not remember whether her feet descended first, or if she appeared to me all at once, whole, in the queer, candied light.

As she floated down to the marble Mary—adorned in the usual sky-blue robe—she imitated the statue's coquettish grin.

I laughed with pure delight! Her feet touched the floor with a slight thud, and then she crouched down and touched my forehead.

"Zoe," she said.

I sat up.

"Is it you?" I asked.

She nodded. Her fingers were a shade cold, but she smelled of Christmas cookies, and the sound of my childhood name warmed me. She took my hand and wasted no time in telling me her request. The Virgin Mary wanted a medal struck in her honor.

"This is how I would like the medal to appear, Zoe." She cast her eyes to the floor. When she looked up, the space where her pupil and iris had been in her left eye now showed the letter M intertwining the cross; in her right eye were two hearts, one crowned and one pierced with a sword, against a background of stars.

I stared into her eyes, memorizing the patterns, then nodded. Mary blinked and her eyes returned to their previous cocoa brown. Just for that second I studied her face. She was very beautiful, but in a regular way. She had pores.

"Whoever wears the medal in good faith shall receive great graces from God," she said.

Then, reading my heart, she agreed that the silences imposed at the convent were silly. In direct opposition to Sister Clare, she said that idle chatter did, in fact, please God immensely. She confessed that she loved to talk for hours on end. And though the Bible claimed she told no one about the visit from the Archangel Gabrielle heralding her immaculate conception, that was not true. Long before she told Joseph, she had told her mother.

"Mama alternately flew about the house screaming, 'No! It's asking too much of you!' and then hugging me close to her, telling me she knew I was a special girl, always." Mary sighed blissfully, and shut her eyes.

I felt a stab of jealousy, thinking of the glory of her life. Mary. The Queen of the Universe. The mother of the savior being comforted by her own sainted mother was just too much for me. I inventoried my sorry life: my mother dying in my girlhood, the lonely life at home with my father, my sister's recent betrayal and other miseries at Saint Vincent de Paul.

The Blessed Mother looked up at the altar, at the carved naked Jesus languishing on the cross, his head twisted in sensual agony.

Mary frowned. "I've certainly never cared for that pose."

"I've always hated it, too. When I was a child it made me weep."

"You can't imagine how it felt to see him—my baby!—all strung up like that." She brought her hand to her mouth." Given a choice, I would never have given my son up for a cause. Of course, when the archangel Gabrielle appeared to me, he didn't tell me I would someday see my son tortured. You can be quite sure he left out that little tidbit. But Zoe, God is good. I've known such happiness in my life. I have known ecstasy. But the crucifixion! I can't let it go. Oh, How I longed to fly unto the cross and cover his beaten body with my own." Mary looked around the dismal chapel, at the peeling walls, the wax posies on the altar, the scarred wooden floor that carried the smell of standing water.

"Zoe Laboure," she said, and kissed my hand with such tenderness that my anxieties vaporized. "I know a girl's life is hard." She waved her hands at the statue of her likeness, and then at her son on the cross. "I still don't know why all these strange things happened to me. I was a regular girl. Why was it me?"

"Oh Mary," I said, emboldened by the Blessed Mother's own questions, "why did God take my mother when she was so young?" I meant when *I* was so young. "What about his infinite mercy?"

Mary's eyes filled with tears. Perhaps I had expected that she would say God had spirited away my mother because he wanted to enjoy her kindness and humor, but seeing my perpetual suffering, he realized his error and would have her resurrected in approximately three days, or that Mary would raise her left hand toward the heavens and oh, a miracle far sweeter than seeing the Blessed Mother—my own mother would float down to me.

Mary took my hand and whispered, "So many mysteries of faith have not been revealed to me. I'm sorry, Zoe. I know how hard it is to be the one left behind."

She kissed me again, then stood on tiptoe and floated off the floor.

"Zoe, an M intertwining a cross and two hearts, one forever crowned and one forever pierced." The translucent cone of pink light appeared, surrounding her again. "Stars float in the background."

When she raised her hand to wave goodbye, black licorice whips sprouted from her fingertips and dropped on the chapel floor. As I puzzled over that, she continued her pinata wave, and fat, peppered shrimp fell from the soft skin between her thumb and forefinger.

"Bye, Zoe Laboure," she called down to me.

I blanketed the bottom of my robe to catch the hot fish.

As she ascended further, laughing, her bare feet split open, revealing bright layers of tightly furled daffodils blossoms that bloomed as they showered upon me.

And then she was gone. I sat on the wooden floor and devoured the shrimp. I had last eaten peppered shrimp with my mother, on my seventh birthday. When she arrived home with the shrimp still sizzling beneath the butcher paper, we caved in to temptation and did not save it for dinner. We ate on the front porch, sucking our burned fingers. In the yard the year's first daffodils bloomed earlier than usual, because, my mother said, it was my birthday. Just as I swallowed the last bite of shrimp, she produced two sticks of black licorice from the pocket of her skirt. I crushed up against her soft body as I ate the candy. With my mouth full of sugar, and the fresh air smelling faintly of my mother's goat's milk soap, dreamy happiness swelled inside my body like a thousand blooms. But then I had a terrible feeling of desperation, already missing the sweetness of the moment, though I had not moved one inch and my mother was now massaging the crown of my head with her fingertips.

She cupped my chin in her hand, "What's wrong, birthday girl?"

The Virgin Mary's remembrance of this scene from my childhood relieved my adult loneliness. I had someone to watch over me.

Now I'm swabbing your back with Bactine. I feel your muscles tensing. Does it sting? Imagine how beautiful the medallion will be on your back: the M intertwining the cross and the two hearts, one crowned and one pierced, with stars floating in the background. The likeness of the Virgin and the message adorning your mother's medallion are a jeweler's detail. Mary did not request a likeness of herself and the words, *Oh mother protect me,* are sketched in our brains. I know you are not particularly holy, that you feel sheepish about adorning your body with religious symbols. You're the girl who owns pope-on-a rope soap, the girl who wants to start a fast food restaurant serving deep-fried Eucharist wafers cuz' once you taste the crispy, crunchy body of Christ, you just can't stop snacking.

Well.

The morning after Mary's visitation, I rose at four o'clock with the other sisters and went to the chapel to pray the rosary. I'd hidden the daffodils inside my pillow case and a licorice stick was tucked in the arm of my robe. Each time I lowered my mouth to my hands, whispering prayers into my rosary beads, I took a bite of my private Eucharist. At dawn, as the last nub of licorice melted on my tongue, the sun shot a gleaming ray through the patched hole in the roof, illuminating a yellow petal in front of the altar.

"Blessed art thou among women!" I screamed, "and blessed is the fruit of thy womb Jesus!"

As the other sisters turned to stare at me, I laughed with ecstasy, fearing I might ascend to the chapel ceiling like Mary. I marveled at their innocence and longed to tell them the truth about my joy. But jealousy abounded at Saint Vincent de Paul—many sisters were hell-bent on sainthood. I knew the visitation from Mary would create an inferno of envy, so I confided only in the parish priest from my childhood. He believed me, and appealed to the bishop, who appealed to the archbishop, who appealed to one of the Pope's henchman, who appealed to the Pope. The medal was struck.

After this interlude, I faded into a life of submission and duty. I learned to care for the sick and dying, though I questioned God's impulse for cruelty, especially in the case of children. I prayed for Louisa to love me as she had when we were children, but her heart was too full of the Father, Son, and Holy Spirit. I prayed that I might love Jesus Christ, but I could only conjure a modest adoration for our savior. It was Mary that I loved, not the icon of purity, but the Mary who revealed herself in the chapel: She was supposed to be the cheerleader for the whole deal, but in her immaculate heart she felt bitterness, for she had not wanted her son to suffer. Whether I was happily strolling through the spring gardens at Saint Vincent de Paul, touching the soft skins of tulips and breathing the fertile air, or clenched with rheumatism, scrubbing the stone floors on a thundery day, I felt the presence of the Blessed Mother.

I'm ready to start. Don't flinch! So, you say that piercing your nose was exquisitely painful, that you hate even getting a flu shot. Interesting. I'm not claiming that your nose ring didn't sting, but consider the suffering of the martyred girl saints: Agnes raised her neck to the sword; Lucy ripped out her eyes; Agatha let the Roman soldiers lop off her breasts. In comparison, a tattoo is an angel's kiss. And the modern tattoo gun is a wonder. After a few seconds of discomfort, your body adjusts to the rhythmic movement of the needle. Then, all you feel is a warm, electric buzz.

But I see this news disappoints you. You wanted the pain. You wanted to make your suffering tangible, say, a broken bone, a shard of glass in your eye, the swelter of a fresh tattoo. This would never match the agony of your new and everlasting loneliness. Walking past the gun shop this morning, you had to wonder: would there be a second, suspended between this world and the next, where you listened to your cochleas' screaming, your skull crumbling like marzipan? You need the tattoo of the miraculous medallion to serve a visible sign of the Blessed Mother's love, to remind you that she watches over you, to remind you that I, Zoe, watch over you, that I feel the zoom of your giddy days and labor over your sad days, that I have examined your trials and found them interesting and that I have loved you in my distant, saintly way.

And tattooed to your skin, the medallion will never be lost or tossed away, like your mother's. The winter of her senior year in high school, your mother held the medal between her thumb and forefinger, sliding it back and forth on the thin silver chain, praying. She prayed for blood, a thousand prayers, until the entire day became a prayer, each sheet corner tucked into the mattress, every algebra problem solved, every time she pulled a brush through her hair: *Oh Gracious Mother, I didn't even like him, I hardly knew him, Hail Mary, full of Grace, the Lord is with thee, I'd drunk four vodka tonics, never was it known that anyone who fled to your protection, implored your help, or sought your intercession was left unaided.*

She pressed her fingers to the medallion, and prayed, please Blessed Mother, give me my life. And still the blood did not come. After her fateful doctor's appointment, your mother drove out to Lake Okaboji. She parked her car and roamed the snowy beach. The water was shallow where it banked so jumping was not an option. But walking into one's own watery death had a pleasing Joan of Arc quality. She imagined the drowsy pleasure of dying, before her body, the secret of her body, became nothing more than a pretty husk in a satin casket.

Your mother yanked the necklace off by the medallion, yelled, "Thanks for nothing, bitch," and sailed it into the lake. Then, waving her hands over her head and screaming, she closed her eyes and scrambled down the bank into the water.

The freezing shock made her turn back, her arms flailing towards the beach, but she tripped and crashed down in the water, and her long, white parka swallowed what seemed like half the lake. The weight of her new prayers *oh why, why, if Jesus could cure lepers and make the blind see, why didn't he help me Blessed Mother help me now* pulled her down, and yards of white fake-fur sucked her down, down, and the flat lake water swelled into a fast icy wave, pulling her down.

Your mother tried to unzip the coat but her fingers had stiffened from the cold, and the heavy hem closed around her ankles. She wiggled her arms from the sleeves and pulled the parka over her head—the sensation of wrestling a polar bear—freeing herself. But when she jumped up, she crashed right back into the water; an icy sludge of mud had glued her boots to the lake's bottom. Saving herself meant total immersion: Taking a deep breath, she squeezed her eyes shut, and plunged into the dark and glacial cold. Bracing her hands on the top of her boots, she pulled her feet out, then rose easily from the water, and in her stocking feet, crying, tripped back up the bank.

Snow crunched under her feet sharp as glass and her ponytail froze into an icicle as your mother ran to her car. With numb hands she opened the door—leaving a strip of bloody skin on the chrome handle—started the engine, stripped off her icy-cold clothes and pressed her toes to the heat vents on the dash. She grabbed a spiral notebook from the back seat and hugged it to her bare chest as she watched her parka float across the lake.

One week later an ice fisherman caught a ten-pound northern pike. When he cleaned it, his knife scraped up on your mother's medallion. Would you believe that his wife ate the fish and completely recovered from breast cancer?

But holy mysteries eluded your mother. For her, there was nine months of pregnancy, the excruciating miracle of birth, the wariness of caring for a newborn. Then, one morning the next winter, she pushed your stroller along the snowy beach of Lake Okaboji. The paddle boats were docked at the lagoon, and your mother envisioned the two of you, in matching green bikinis, going for a ride the next summer. With the last ten pounds of her pregnancy weight gone she would be sleek as a cat. She put the brake on your stroller and sat at a picnic table thinking about her dreary job at the office supply store; she envied her friends off at college, free to smoke pot and eat carrot cake at will while she washed diapers and sold staplers. But then she looked down at you. She remembered that terrible day, the pull of the water all around her. She kissed your mittened hand. *I didn't know how much I would love you,* she whispered. The sun flared out over the frozen lake, and you were squinting at the bright whiteness. Ice crystals fringed your dark eye lashes, and when you turned your worried, jeweled gaze to your mother, she gasped. Exhilarated by your baby beauty, joy suddenly rushed through her, and your mother picked you up and held your face to hers. The north wind had carved your cheeks into blistery roses. *My baby* your mother cried, and plunged you into the air over her head.

Though her exhilaration warmed you, you felt dizzy, and your new brain formed the thought: Oh mother, protect me.

You're nodding now, you are ready for your tattoo. It is kind of you to submit. And you're smiling like a believer, like I can rid you of all your miseries. My original idea was that the medallion tattooed to your skin might leech away all sadness, pull it out of your heart, so you could always be happy. But I am a minor saint, and there is no cure for sorrow. A girl's life is an endless pilgrimage of joy and grief. All I can give you is the tattoo of the miraculous medallion, without pain or swelling. I'm taking off these latex gloves. Yes, I'm putting the tattoo gun down now. When you walk out of Zoe's Exotic Skin Arts you will have the medallion on your back, a glory beneath your clothes. My saint's trick, my minor miracle, is that I need no needles, no cotton to blot the blood as I work. In this second, as I press my palm on your back, the Mother's love is made visible. Feel it now, on your skin, an M intertwining the cross and the two hearts, one crowned and one pierced. Stars float in the background.

The Patron Saint of Travelers

The heat in our small room is a surprise. I thought London would be gray and cool, melancholy and rainy, even in August, but probably I got that idea from the movies. Lying here next to me on an ancient mattress is my best friend Calla Delaney. We've concocted a garbage bag sheet because the mattress is covered with tiny hairs and scary, paisley-shaped stains.

"Jane! Jesus!" Calla screams, jolting up on her elbows. "The bags on the bottom half are shifting! My calves are on the bare mattress and it's boiling hot and I'm sweating like a pig which means my pores are open, sucking up the freaky body juice from all the other freaks who've slept here. Yiah!"

She jumps up shaking her arms and legs like she's covered with snakes. My legs are on the bare mattress, but I can't get up because I'm laughing so hard—Calla's phrase "freaky body juice." Plus, we are high.

Our new roommate Alice pokes her head through the door and flips the light switch. She's wearing a Sarah Lawrence T-shirt and a puzzled, irritated expression that may in fact be her regular face.

"Why is that mattress such a trial for you two?" Alice asks.

"It's hairy!" Calla yells, hopping around the room. "It's sex-stained!"

Alice leans against the wall raking her hand through her blonde ponytail. "Since the epidermis continually rejuvenates itself, we're all inhaling each other's skin flakes," she says. "We're all losing hairs, sweating, secreting fluids; we're all actively involved in this business of being human."

"But, Alice, it's so hot," I say. "Are you sure you don't have an extra sheet or a tablecloth or anything?"

"A tablecloth? I travel light." She smirks at the junk Calla and I have heaped against the wall: clothes, suitcases, camera bags, five cartons of duty-free Marlboros, a powder blue Samsonite make-up case my mother purchased for her honeymoon in 1961, a box of Tide that traveled across the sea with us, Calla's Clairol 24 hot curlers, Cadbury roses, passports with a special stamp allowing us to work legally for six months, and London guide books that we apparently don't need.

After landing at Heathrow yesterday and going through customs, we struggled outside with our luggage and shared a cigarette at the taxi stands. We couldn't find the paper we'd written the addresses of hostels on, but the cabdriver who picked us up didn't find it odd that we didn't know where to go, or that we held hands and cried in the back seat: After all our daydreaming, we had made it to London. He drove us to Sloane Square, our new neighborhood, to see a woman who rents apartments to vacationers and students.

Alice's eyes linger on the curlers. "I can carry all my belongings in a backpack."

"Jesus, how wonderful for you! Houdini lives!" I say boldly, because my heart is thumping from the heart-shaped speed Calla and I bought from a man playing guitar on Tottenham Court Road. Ms. Genius Alice thinks owning electric curlers, which Calla uses to coax her fabulously string-straight red hair into a Veronica Lake, is a personality defect.

"Why do you have to be like that, Jane?" Alice whines, backing out of our room. "It's not my fault I don't have an extra sheet. I'm not a damn linen store."

Calla and I arrange the garbage bags again, and put T-shirts down where two pillows would normally be on a bed. The only other furnishing in the room is a maple wardrobe full of mementos abandoned by previous tenants: a frayed paperback copy of *Frannie and Zooey*, (Upon discovery we bowed to the book; we wrote to J.D. Salinger after reading *Catcher in the Rye* our junior year in high school, then watched our mail boxes like war brides), a jumble of Silk Cut cartons and Smartie wrappers, a purple acrylon dress from the Top Shop, and a diaphragm. This last artifact I picked up and cradled in my palm, perplexed—Calla and I are on the pill—until I realized what I was holding and screamed. Calla threw open the window and I flung it outside and, then, shrouded by the dirty curtains, we leaned on the window sill and watched the diaphragm flutter to the ground like a rubber shooting star.

As soon as I flip off the light and we try the mattress again, Calla laughs. "I'm sorry, Janie, it's your hair! You're your own personal night light. It looks fabulous, though."

I scramble around on the floor until I find my compact. "Oh, shit. I'm phosphorescent."

Yesterday Calla and I took our first walk on King's Road, grooving on the beauty that is suddenly our life. I stopped at a salon and had my shoulder-length brown hair cut to my chin and bleached until my scalp burned, until my hair was the hue and texture of dental floss.

"Hey Jane, remind me to get one of those electrical converters for my curlers tomorrow."

"Sure," I say, looking at her profile in the half-light from the window, at her mouth which opens and closes in fish-like palpitations.

"Janie, can you believe we made it here?"

In February, Calla and I saw a poster in the student lounge of Kansas City Community College that said: Work In Europe! We dropped our classes immediately and worked double shifts at The Golden Ox to save money.

"It's like a dream. Not the kind where you run through a field of flowers with the sun streaming down your back, but a dream so bizarre that even while you're sleeping, you're conscious of the dream's strangeness."

"Mmm" Calla says, biting her lip now, tapping her fingers along her thighs. "Anyway, why are we trying to sleep in the first place? We're still buzzing from the speed."

"Please don't talk about it. I think my heart's going to stop. I think I'm never going to sleep again. I'm homesick even though I never want to go home again."

"God, me too. Let's walk down to the pay phones."

We throw dresses over our T-shirts, debating whether the time here is six hours earlier or later than home. This is not a huge problem. Break of dawn or middle of the night, everyone will be happy to hear from us. The last time one of our relatives traveled to a different continent their destination was Ellis Island.

Before we tiptoe to the door, Calla writes 24 Draycott Place on the inside of her forearm with a red marker. Our new address.

I stand on the front step of our apartment building holding the bag of samosas and the cokes we bought at the Chelsea Kitchen—thrilling at all the people walking down the street—and return the smile of a guy with a rockabilly bouffant, happy that beautiful Calla has her back turned, unlocking the big double doors. Though it looks like the grandest mansion from the street, the inside is ratty with sooty walls and threadbare rose-colored carpet.

Calla frowns into the scratched mirror hanging in the foyer. "It's nice to know how I'll look at forty," she says, because we haven't slept in days and we're looking road weary.

We take the three flights of stairs to our apartment and hear Alice crying as we walk in the door. She's stretched out on the kitchen floor on her sleeping bag, yelling, "I can't believe this shit, Simone! I can't believe you're this inconsiderate!"

Calla and I slink by, offering her awkward half-smiles and nods, then walk past her room where a shirtless man sits on her mattress, smoking. His jeans are unbuttoned at the waist. When we say hello, he grins in a bored sort of way. In our own room we find a petite, dark-haired girl wearing an orange peignoir and eighteen-hole Doc Martin's, rifling through the junk in the wardrobe.

"Goddamnit to hell," she says to us, "I can't find my diaphragm."

"Is that right?" I hug the bag of food to my chest.

"We're your new roommates, I think," Calla says, extending her hand.

"Yeah, yeah," she says, ignoring Calla's hand, "lovely to meet you and all that. I've been using this room since the last girls moved out. Which has been nice, because Alice and I have been paying only twelve pounds per week to have our own rooms. I suppose all good things must come to an end." She gets on her hands and knees and runs her hand underneath the wardrobe. "You haven't by chance seen a diaphragm have you?"

Calla very coolly says, "Unfortunately, we tossed it out the window."

"What the fuck?" Simone says, standing up. "What'd you go and do that for? Are you fucking loony?"

"Sorry, but how were we supposed to know?" Calla puts her hand on her hip. "The landlady said we could toss out anything we found in the room."

"The landlady said we could toss out anything we found in the room," Simone says with a twangy American accent, startling us with her meanness. "Oh, it's one fucking thing after another for old Simone. I should kill myself. I should jump right out the fucking window."

"Listen," I say, "you should thank us. It was in a pile of candy wrappers in this hot room. There was probably a ton of freaky bacteria growing on it."

Calla nods. "You were begging for an infection."

From the next room, the man calls out, "Simone?"

She pounds on the wall and yells, "Just fuck off for a minute."

In the kitchen, Alice sniffles.

"What's wrong with Alice?" Calla asks.

"She just got the boot from this fellow named Kevin. They spent the night together a few times and dummy Alice started thinking they were soul mates, when really Kevin was an Australian on holiday. I can't be bothered." She takes a cigarette from one of our packs on the floor and lights it with a pearlized lighter she pulls from the top of her boot. "Ah, American Marlboros," she says, exhaling.

"Where are you from?" Calla asks. "You have such a pretty accent."

"Auckland. *New Zealand.* Listen, girls. Do you really think I might have an infection from the diaphragm? Now that you've brought it up, I'm quite a bit worried."

"I'm sure you're fine," I say, looking for a place to set the food.

"Oh I'm sure I'm *not* fine. I'm probably burning up with infection as we speak." Simone paces back and forth in the tiny space between the mattress and the wardrobe, banging her forehead with the back of her hand. "I shouldn't even be worrying about this. Christ, I don't know *why* I'm letting the penis rule me! I don't know why I've made the penis my fucking king!"

She storms into the next room and stage-whispers, "you may as well fucking go."

Calla and I can't look at each other. We laugh silently, bent over at the waist, until we feel lightheaded.

"Let's eat," Calla whispers. "I'm weak."

We kneel at the end of the mattress and use the window sill as a table. Alice continues to cry, her pillow-muffled sobs echoing through the apartment. I think of creeping into the kitchen to talk to her, but remember how mean she'd been to us when we moved in, how snobby. "I'm sure your first trip to Europe will be highly instructional," she'd said, then bragged about how she'd lived on every continent because her parents were renowned violinists. Bore me later. Instead of helping us move our stuff in, she'd sat at the kitchen table hurling puzzling insults: "I assume you'll want to visit Buckingham Palace. Maybe take a tour of Harrod's? Perhaps you'll enjoy a day at Stratford-upon-Avon?"

While Cal and I eat, we flip through a copy of the *Daily Mirror*, stopping at a picture of Charles and Diana holding hands in front of a horse stable. Unbelievably, he's wearing knee-length plaid shorts and knee socks. Diana looks frowny and depressed. She's been married to him for four years, since she was nineteen, the age Calla and I are now.

"Screw the money and getting to be a princess," I say.

"No shit. Can you imagine being trapped inside a castle with him?"

There's a staggered, breathy cry from the next room, the sound of bodies shifting on the mattress.

Calla bows her head. "All hail the king."

At ten in the morning we're on the underground, the Northern line, headed for Camden Town. Calla's twisted around in her seat, trying to catch her reflection in the window as she applies lipstick. A girl sitting across from us is wearing a blood-red dress with iridescent black stockings and white patent leather t-straps. Slung over her shoulder is a purse, tiny as a child's, that matches her shoes.

When Calla turns around, I jab my head in the girl's direction. "I'm throwing all my clothes in the trash."

"I know," she whispers, "I love that outfit. God! Don't you wish you knew every single person on the train? What their house looks like, what kind of job they have, are they heartbroken? Do they get high?"

I point to the map of the underground next to the double doors. "And every black dot is it's own world with a million cool shops and clubs and people we'll never know unless we stop there."

"And this is only one line," Calla says, and with our hearts fluttering we stare at the bright squiggling lines, each representing a train that shuttles through London, and at the color-coded key with their pretty names: Jubilee, Victoria, Picadilly, Bakerloo.

As the train pulls into the Camden Town station a booming voice announces, "Mind the gap." We jump off the train and nearly fall into the space between the train and the cement platform. Stepping outside the station is like crashing into heaven. Vendors line the streets in all directions, their booths packed with food and paintings and junk and clothes and jewelry and bootleg cassettes, and the air smells like gasoline and wilting roses. Calla and I stand still, shading our eyes, unsure of where to go.

"This way." Calla pulls me over to a table adjacent to the station, where people sign petitions and drop change into a pale green bucket that says: SUPPORT THE MINERS.

"Excuse me," she says to the guy sitting behind the table.

He smiles up at her. Despite the heat he's wearing a black leather jacket. His hair, dyed licorice- black, falls over his forehead and curtains his eyes which are the loony, astonished blue of the saints in Catholic art.

She smiles back, dropping her eyelids coquettishly. "Mmm, I wonder if you could tell me about the miners. Because my father is a miner. In America. In West Virginia"

Calla's father sells car insurance in Kansas. I set my mouth in a grim, depressed line to keep from laughing.

"Oh, lovely." he says. "We've had a lot of support from our friends in West Virginia, from Pittman." He explains how Margaret Thatcher's greed is ravaging the mining industry while studying Calla's face. I look at her poreless skin and trace my finger over pebbles of acne on my chin.

"There's a miner's benefit tonight at the Hackney Empire," he finally says, handing Calla a red flyer. "My band's playing. I hope you can make it."

"How kind of you to invite us," Calla says.

We walk casually away from the booth, threading our way through swarms of people. Calla slaps at my arm as I quietly sing "Country Roads, take me home, to the place I belong, West Virginia." As soon as we turn the corner she screams, "Jackpot," and waves the red flyer over her head.

"Calla, he's not even a miner. He's a musician trying to get some lovin'."

"Now, Jane, that's really no way to talk about my future husband." She links her arm through mine.

We follow a crowd into a crumbly old building where the coolness and cheapness of all the merchandise makes us pant, and buy identical black dresses and pointy shoes the Wicked Witch of the West would envy.

A rickety table at the back of the building is empty except for one wooden box of bootleg cassettes. The teenage boy behind the table is crouched on a Marshall amplifier. With the spikes of his mohawk dyed deep aqua and purple he looks cheery, festive as a parrot, but he is an aloof salesman who completely ignores us while he reads the *New Musical Express*. Calla nods at me like we might be looking at a good opportunity. We've vowed to stop indulging in drugs at age 21, at which point we may pursue a career in airport security. We flip through the cassettes for a long time until I finally just ask if he's selling anything else.

He keeps reading while he separates four tabs of Felix the Cat acid from a sheet stuck between the pages of the paper, drops them in an empty cassette box and hands it to me.

"Ten quid," he says, looking past us.

Calla hands him the money and offers a cheerful thanks. He makes a brusque gesture which may mean either good-bye or get the hell away.

I'm paranoid that he's a junior officer of Scotland Yard about to pull off his mohawk wig, which is why I don't figure out the math until we're walking back to the train. In accordance with the Dating Law of the World, we return a different way to avoid the awkwardness of seeing Calla's miner/musician before tonight. The street we're on now is residential and strangely deserted; the revelry only a block away filters to a pleasant buzz. We pass boarded-up buildings with the words 'Post No Bills' painted above bright posters advertising bands and SUPPORT THE MINERS signs.

"My God, Calla, we just paid fourteen dollars for four hits of acid."

"That guy's got the best job in the world. Just sitting there reading, selling a product he probably really believes in."

A muffled voice calls out, "hello hello oh hello."

We spin around looking in every direction, until Calla points at a building across the street. "Look! The window on the top floor."

A small girl, silhouetted by the window screen, is waving at us. We put our bags on the sidewalk and wave our hands in the air over our heads, a big movement, like we are landing planes.

Tonight Calla and I wore our matching black dresses from the market. We worried we would look like back-up singers in a country band, but the Hackney Empire, this stately old theater packed with miners and punk-rockers, was so dark and smoke-filled you could hardly see. Right now I'm clenching the hem of my dress. I'm riding in a car driven by a person named David. He's driving on the wrong side of streets I'm seeing for the first time. In the side mirror, my hair glows as shockingly white as snowball hydrangea seen by the light of the moon. I'm reeling from two hits of acid—every time I glance at David his new face bends into a mutation of the last one.

If I concentrate hard enough, surely all these facts will snap into a logical pattern.

"I could tell you girls were Americans right away," David says.

There's a delay in the conversation while I'm busy matching up his comment with the sequence of time to which it belongs. David played in the same band as Jimmy, Calla's friend from Camden Town. After they finished their set, Jimmy spotted Calla, and he and David sat with us at a round table by the stage. People shook their hands and asked for autographs.

"Are they a little bit famous?" Calla whispered.

"Let's put it this way, Cal. If you weren't a groupie before, consider yourself one now."

She ruffled my bangs. "Yeah, well you've got the hair for it, blondie."

Now David turns the corner too quickly and time freezes as we skid.

"Oh sorry. The streets are a bit wet. Anyway, I could tell you were Americans because of your teeth."

"Is that right?"

"Because generally Americans have nice teeth."

"Right. That's right. I mean, no. I have terrible teeth; they're all filled. The dentist says I breathe cavities because my teeth are porous as a sponge." I round my back and turn away from him, running my fingertips over my front teeth.

"Well, they look quite nice."

"Thank you," I say.

We drive along in silence. I'm panicky, sitting in what should be the driver's seat; periodically I think I'm forgetting to drive and that we're about to crash. I stomp my foot on a non-existent brake, trying to stop this death mobile, grabbing at the air where the steering wheel should be.

After a zillion eternitys he parks the car and walks around to my side to let me out. Five points, I think.

"Where are we?" I ask, stretching my hands over my head. All I see are the backs of buildings, their zigzaggy stairs and cat walks.

"Seven Sisters."

"That's a pretty name. I wish I lived in Seven Sisters."

"Where do you live?"

"A street called Draycott Place. The tube stop is Sloane Square." He takes my hand and we walk through a muddy yard and up a rickety fire escape. I try not to look down at the stairs, which are composed of air and the occasional wooden strip.

"Central London. You should move north. It's a nicer place to live."

"Calla and I have only been in London three days. I don't know north from central from south from east," I say, carving an elaborate diagram in the air with my hand and then, mesmerized, watching the glowing white lines left in their wake.

At the top of the second set of stairs he unlocks the door, then turns to me. "Thank you for coming home with me, Jane."

"Oh, no problem," I say brightly, which makes us both laugh.

He opens the door and steps back to let me go in first. But the misty night air feels so clean and I don't know him from Jack, and I'm not a nun but I've only had sex with four people so I'm not the slut of Satan either. I see the high ceilings are painted butter cream and that Margaret Thatcher's face is pinned to a dart board in a foyer—boy, people really do not like her—and I think that I'd always like to be standing here on the fire escape wearing my new dress, waiting for the next moment.

Then he touches the small of my back and I walk in. The room is uncluttered, with just a bed by the window and guitars and guitar cases on the floor.

"Would you like a cup of tea?" he asks.

"No." I laugh, because who drinks tea but old people? "Do you like tea?"

He nods, raising my chin with his finger; we kiss quickly, like friends.

He whispers, "Are you sure you want to do this?"

"Yes," I say, panicky, "don't you?"

He laughs, pulling me close to him and we undress and move to the bed. Just like that, I am in London, naked. The sex is okay but I have to fight the sensation that his skin is composed of candle wax, that my fingers will sink down to the first knuckle when I touch him. I ricochet from crashing happiness to heartbreak and back to joy before I start feeling ruined again, my heart crucified and resurrected a thousand times before the clock radio changes from 3:25 to 3:26.

Then I think to ask where the bathroom is, but I'm so exhausted I can't form the words. With his breath on my neck and the acid still working behind my eyes, I am a medical oddity, a pilgrim: I fall asleep.

★ ★ ★

We wake to the silvery clanging of church bells and David drives me home. My head aches from the snakebites I guzzled at the Hackney Empire, and the inside of my mouth is like a sour old metal medicine chest. With sadness I think of my parents day-dreaming about me, wondering if I'm at a play, or a museum, or touring Westminster Abbey.

He lets the car idle on the corner of Draycott Place. He kisses my hand.

"It was wonderful to meet you, Jane." he says.

"You too," I say. A long second passes where he does not suggest that we meet again. I am a swirl of wrinkled clothes, smeared make-up and bed-head, so I don't make eye contact; I just get out of the car. As I stand on the curb waving good-bye he unrolls the passenger window and sticks out his fist.

"This is for you," he says. "Good luck."

"Thank you," I say, holding out my hand.

Then I can tell simply by the feel of metal and rough edges he has given me a British coin. Have I just been paid one coin for sex? Perhaps he has simply tipped me. He drives off slowly, smiling at me in his rear view mirror, checking for my reaction, I guess. I smash the coin into my palm with my finger-tips, hurting my hand as I run up the steps of 24 Draycott Place. I sit on the top step and hang my head between my knees, try-ing to think about nothing at all.

"Janie," I hear Calla call, alarm buzzing her voice, "what's wrong?"

Her pointed black shoes cripple her run but she's still

moving fast in her wrinkled dress, with her purse and long, red hair shooting behind her.

"Nothing," I yell. I look across the street at the attached buildings standing together like skinny castles and at the black taxis on the street, and at Calla, the miracle of Calla coming down Draycott Place. I live in London with my best friend and it is summer. So screw David Holcomb. But as I open my hand to look at the coin before I fling it down the steps, a burst of relieved joy flowers my heart. I am holding a Saint Christopher medal.

"You're okay," Calla says, climbing the steps. "Nothing freaky happened?"

"No, no. Everything's fine. David just dropped me off." I slip the medal in my dress pocket. Christopher. The patron saint of travelers.

"Dropped you off?" She sits down next to me and pulls off her shoes. "Jesus, I took the train. It took about two hours and was confusing as hell. It's a good thing I'm a clever kind of gal," she says grimly.

"Yep," I say. David Holcomb. Saint Christopher. They meld together in my mind, someone to watch over me, something I didn't even know I wanted. I imagine finding red roses on the steps of 24 Draycott Place, a note jammed in the door: *Dear Jane, when can I see you again?*

Calla stares over at me harshly, and says, "Well Calla, how was your night? Did anything freaky happen to you?"

I ignore her snappiness because of the Saint Christopher medal in my pocket, because the world is always twisting so.

"I'm sorry, Calla. How *was* your night?" I wipe away a mascara smudge under her eye.

"No, I'm sorry, it's just that my night was so messed up. Jimmy took me to his house in Clapham—where were you?"

"Seven sisters."

Like the college? So, whatever, everything is fine, we're having some beers, I mean lagers—*not beers, love, lagers*—except, God, he lives with his zombie mother."

"Mr. Cool Guy Musician lives with his mom?"

"We walk in at three in the morning and she's sitting there in her puffy red robe watching TV and she doesn't even say hello—not like I'm dying to have some big conversation with her—so anyway we go down to his apartment in the basement, and end up having sex. Sort of, he's pretty drunk, and I'm half grooving on my druggy little adventure and half wondering why I play these reindeer games, when someone knocks on the basement door. It's his friend Richard, from the bar, and Jimmy brings him downstairs even though I'm naked in the bed, and says, 'Richard thinks you're unbelievable, would you mind if Richard got in bed with you?'"

"Mr. Help-The-Miners is asking you to have sex with his friend?"

"Except I don't have to humor him like I would a psychopath because old Mom upstairs might save me if I scream.

I flat out tell him there's no way in hell that little scenario is going to take place, so Richard leaves and Jimmy sits on the side of the bed, naked, playing guitar and pouting, and I just have to sink under the dirty sheets and wait for the sun to come up so I can leave."

"Mr. We-On-The-Left-Have-The-Moral-High-Ground traps you like a rat at his house."

"Okay, that's getting on my last nerve," Calla says.

"Well, I want you to know you weren't having some kind of perception problem because he seemed nice earlier."

"I guess it's the same all over the world, Jane. If you're equal and willing guys have to pull some fucking power play to humiliate you."

"That's so true." I say it with conviction so she won't notice me floating in a pink fairy bubble of love for Saint David Holcomb.

"Anyway, I've had it with the boys and the drugs. Tomorrow we've got to get the paper and start looking for jobs and find a Laundromat and a grocery store, but for right now let's just go get some damn lunch."

We go to the Chelsea kitchen for hamburgers. Beefburgers, they call them. Beefburgers! Nothing is more hilarious.

When we get home from lunch we find Simone sitting at the kitchen table smoking cigarettes with a policeman.

"Girls," he says, standing up, "I'm very sorry to have to tell you that your roommate Alice Jenkins has committed suicide." He bows his head and holds his cigarette behind his back.

"S'alright," Simone sighs, touching his arm. "they've just moved in."

"Was it just now?" I ask stupidly.

"About an hour ago," the policeman says, sitting back down.

"Out the window she went," Simone says, "I've just had a ferocious fight with the ambulance men, because they said she certainly died on impact. And well, she didn't, did she? I was just in here making some tea and I heard her open the window, and then I heard a falling noise."

"A falling noise?" Calla says.

"Alice didn't jump out far enough," Simone says. "She scraped against the front of the building as she went down." She covers her mouth for a second. "I went to the bedroom and looked out the window and she was on her back, with one of her legs twisted in the hedges. I screamed out her name and she groaned. She was wearing her bathrobe. She was getting ready to have a bath."

The policeman pats Simone on the back and looks up at us. "Could one of you please look for her passport? The embassy will need it."

And so we creep into Alice's bedroom, which already has the spooky-museum look of a dead person's room. On the unmade bed the wind flutters pages of a blue spiral notebook and a bag from The Body Shop. Calla opens the bag gingerly and pulls out a bottle of Dewberry bath oil and the receipt.

"She bought it today," Calla says, "so the jump must have been an impulse."

I flip through the notebook and find her unsent letters to Kevin. I read them aloud to Calla, feeling guilty and hopeful, as if our intrusiveness might resuscitate Alice, as if she might fly through the window in a rage and grab her notebook. The first letter is a study in breeziness: *Hey Kev, So what's the good word from Perth?* The following letters escalate in despair until the last smeared page: *Dear Kevin, I cannot go on without you..*

"Oh no," I whisper. " You can see if she's living in Winfield, Kansas, working at Burger King and the zit-faced fry cook dumps her. But to toss yourself out the window here?"

I trace my finger over the medallion in my dress pocket, but in a dead girl's room I can't summon the imagination to believe in David Holcomb or Saint Christopher.

"It's not as if we even knew her," Calla says. "But Jesus, can you believe she's dead?"

And I can't, so I imagine Alice recuperating in a full body cast while Calla and I bring her strawberry milk shakes and cigarettes. Calla explains the faulty logic involved in killing yourself over a guy trying to have a memorable vacation while I decorate her cast with silver glitter and red stars. On her leg I write: I survived the summer of 85! Viva Australia! We dust off *Franny and Zooey*, and Calla reads aloud to her: "I can't be running back and forth forever between grief and high delight."

Calla puts both hands on the window sill. "Help me, Jane," she says, pulling one leg up. "I want to see how it looked to her."

"Oh, Calla," I whisper, clapping my hands to her waist.

She pulls her other leg up and squats on the window sill. As she slowly, slowly, raises her body up, I lock my arms around her calves. The curtain blows back, blinding me for a second, and I hold her tighter.

Calla stretches up and braces her arms on the molding above the window. "Jane, "she says, looking down, "hold on to me."

Veronica's Veil

The other women at the shower had purchased bright, comical gifts for baby: a hooded red sleeper sprouting devil ears and a tail, zebra-striped receiving blankets, a jester's cap patterned with green stars and a pair of magenta high-top tennis shoes. But the sonogram had revealed a girl, and it was her best friend's baby, so Veronica bought the loveliest thing she'd ever seen, a tiny, crocheted white coat with five silver buttons that shimmered in the light like sugared disco balls.

"Oh, a little princess coat!" said Gina, pulling it from layers of violet-scented tissue paper. "An angel's coat!"

A bright block of sunshine filtered through the window shades, casting the women ringed around Gina in gauzy, golden, maternal light. Veronica looked around the room, smiling, wondering why she and Gina had befriended this particular collection of witches and wackos.

"Too divine. Of course it would look like a paint smock five minutes after my Zoe had it on," said Lily, their actress friend. She'd cornered Veronica for the first half-hour of the shower, droning on about a feature film she'd landed, detailing the stupidity of her self-absorbed co-stars. When Gina walked by with a platter of creme caramel in scalloped tureens, she and Veronica had exchanged the briefest, comradely smirk.

Joanie, a friend from their rock-and-roll days in the late eighties, touched the soft coat with real alarm, as if Veronica had purchased snow white silicone breasts for the baby to use as teething rings.

"So white!" Joanie said, so superior now with her software engineer husband, Range Rover, and cross-eyed infant sons. She looked at Veronica with the wistfulness of an immigrant moving on, leaving loved ones behind in the slummy old country. Veronica recalled the night Joanie had given one of The Pogues—The lead singer with the broken teeth? The smoldering, angel-eyed drummer?—a blow job backstage at the Beacon Theater, and tried to concoct a lighthearted way to mention it.

When everyone finally went home, Veronica and Gina stuffed wrapping paper and bows into trash bags, loaded the dishwasher, and sat down with the chips and guacamole.

Joanie! Jesus Christ! What had happened to Joanie?

"Miss Thing with all her Prada gear telling me that if I ever get out of the city, Wal-Mart, has 'surprisingly' nice maternity things," Gina said. The baby's due in three weeks and I'm not going on some cut-rate spending spree to look like a big, fat Kathy Lee Gifford."

"Joanie treats me like the poster child for loserdom," Veronica said. "She asked if I still lived in that little place on 103rd and Manhattan Avenue-she knows I do—and then sighed like a Victorian maiden and said, 'I just can't imagine living like that now, but good for you, Veronica.' I hope her husband leaves her for a sixteen-year-old go-go dancer."

"She's jealous because she's stuck with a computer geek and you get sex with a hot musician. Real sex, not get-the-hell-in-bed-I'd-rather-watch-Law-and-Order-too-but-the-ovulation-predictor-kit-shows-a-purple-line sex."

Veronica hadn't told a soul that Dale left over a month ago and now, in Gina's kitchen overlooking West 86th street—the slate blue counter top, the polished hardwood floor—with Gina's globe-stomach bulging beneath her shirt, Veronica saw the weirdness in her secrecy, and also that her world was ending and she was the only one to witness it, Christopher Columbus sailing backwards

And then the father-to-be was home, his key jingling the lock. He carried yellow roses wrapped in a cone of plastic, a husband's cut-rate bouquet purchased at the deli, the petals already softening to sepia.

When he saw Veronica sitting on the couch, he tossed the bouquet on the coffee table like a newspaper and said, "hey, girls."

The roses were just for Gina, not for people to *see* him giving to Gina, and though Veronica knew he was a premature ejaculator and comparison shopped for paper towels, she felt short and sad and injured by loneliness.

The uptown C train stopped in the tunnel between 96th and 103rd street, the sound of a thousand dental drills slowly losing power. The conductor offered a garbled explanation for the delay before cheerfully saying that the metropolitan transit service thanked everyone for their patience. Veronica thought that maybe a dozen years in Manhattan was enough because she didn't consider giving up her seat, even with a man squashed up next to her with his warm, brothy breath at her cheek whispering, "I am not a patient, I am not a patient." He carried a jar of foil-wrapped bouillon cubes that rattled like dice, and he wore latex gloves.

"Which came in handy, because as it turned out he was a doctor, and I was due for a pap-smear, and we were stranded on the train with time to kill." This was what she would tell Dale if Dale still lived at their apartment, and she could live with the illusion that, at age 34, she enjoyed the Bohemian life while her friends retired into domesticity. She envisioned Dale laughing, oh, the squint of his eyes, the specks of glittering eye shadow and liner he never managed to scrub off after nights playing with his glam-rock band, Haley's Glamorama. Well, she'd loved him; she longed to have his baby, Emma or Pauline, Jack or Matthew, longed to walk down Saint Mark's Place with her luscious rock-and-roll husband pushing the carriage. That this would never happen pained her so that she closed her eyes and touched the silver cross she wore on a thin chain around her neck. When the train churned to a screechy crawl, Veronica opened her eyes and saw a Manhattan Woman magazine on the floor, the feature story in blazing orange print above a photo of a luminous teenage model carrying a briefcase: "Is Artificial Insemination The Right Choice For You?"

Divine intervention—it was not the first time she'd sensed it. God was always near, and the girl saints she'd studied in her childhood had never stopped plaguing her—all that fearlessness and devotion and perpetual trust in the sacred heart of Jesus. She picked up the magazine with two fingers, wishing for her own pair of latex gloves, and read. Scientific miracles now rivaled any Biblical story. Keep your loaves and fishes; here is quality sperm Fed-exed to your apartment, asexual reproduction after a quick visit to the doctor. Then you could watch Saturday Night Live in big granddaddy sweat pants while thousands of woman trolled the city wearing slinky skirts and MAC lipstick, hoping. Veronica had hoped to marry Dale at Saint Patrick's Cathedral, wearing her mother dress, with the guests gasping at her beauty, with the Ave Maria swirling from choir loft, with a baby already on the way, a Child of God rising beneath layers of silk shantung. Was the priest blind or liberal? But Dale was Gone. Gone, Daddy, gone. Love has gone away.

Thank God she was a feminist and had options. She wasn't going to wait around, a hopeful hag dolling up to go to the grocery store or taking a fly-fishing class. No, she would join the pioneering women who relied on science, not the penis, to answer their dreams. Tomorrow was Saturday and she would devote the day to researching artificial insemination!

She slept off her bravado and woke early, rode the subway downtown to The Strand and selected a dusty copy of *How to Get Married in One Year or Less*. Standing in the long checkout line, she assumed a bemused, ironic expression as she flipped through the book. Two beautiful twenty-year-old's behind her giggled so hysterically that Veronica smashed the book to her breasts and looked back at the girls with a cool, cat-fight smile. The girls clung to each other like lovers, their black curls crashing around their faces like the darkest waves, the skin under their star-bright eyes a taut and creamy flashback, a pinprick to Veronica's heart: the pre-moisturizer years. Tears burned her eyes as she turned back around, hanging her head. *How to Get Married in One Year or Less.* She would laugh, too, that's the kind of girlie woman she was. But at dawn, as she'd lain in bed clutching Dale's pillow, the stark sorrow of artificial insemination seemed indisputable. She imagined explaining it to her child over cookies and milk: *Mommy didn't know your Daddy. Daddy was just some spermies in a petri dish because Mommy was too much of a big-ass loser to give you an actual human Daddy.* And she thought of her own father at the Girl Scouts Daddy-Daughter picnic, taking his turn in the egg relay. He carried an egg on a spoon, racing to her, his eyes on her and then on the wobbling egg, and then looking back at her with so much hope and anxious love that even in the fifth grade, standing there with her green beret and sash of badges and praying he wouldn't fall on his butt and embarrass her, Veronica believed there would always be a place in the world for her.

Saturday night brought on the usual crushing spell of melancholy. Veronica laid on the futon eating Cup-O-Soup, daydreaming about other lonely people in the city eating salted noodles: a jilted girl at a Columbia dorm huddled over her hot pot, a lonely widower listening to Vivaldi while he ate his soup with a plastic deli spoon, a white-hosed nurse just off her shift at Beth Israel, her feet up on the coffee table, eating in silence. But possibly her silence was due to her husband sleeping in the back bedroom, her beautiful fireman husband: Hey, no soup for you, nursey.

The phone rang and she muted the TV, steeling herself against the blossoming hope it was Dale calling to say *Our love is indestructible. I see that now.* But when the answering machine clicked on, it was her mother back home in Saint Louis, home from Bingo, missing her.

"Roni, are you home? Hello? Dale? Veronica? Oh, okay."

Veronica touched the receiver, but she knew if she picked it up she might break and tell her mother she wanted to move back home, that Dale had fallen in love with a performance artist named Whiskey Jenny.

"Anyway, Veronica, I just wanted to tell you that Daddy and I were out to dinner at the new place where Macelli's used to be—I had the best piece of grilled salmon—and we saw young Father Mike, who was wearing shiny hair gel, real shiny, sweetie, like he'd stuck his head in a vat of crushed diamonds and anyway he was eating with a knock-down gorgeous British man named Wilbur, and I told your Dad, well, bully for him, Father Mike is such a sweetheart, I hate to think of him growing old alone in that depressing rectory and Dad said what the hell's that supposed to mean, and I said it doesn't take a rocket scientist and your dad said why do you always have to assume who is gay and who isn't, and I told him because it's interesting to me, and his homophobia isn't. But later he won 200 dollars at Bingo, so we took the Hamiltons out for margaritas and now everyone's happy. Anyway, Roni, we love you. Sweet dreams."

Oh Mommy, thought Veronica. She ached to pick up the phone and cry: *Why is everything so final ? Why can't I be five again in striped pajamas with everything ahead of me? This time I will play the violin and run track and go to medical school and marry at twenty-five and have two babies by thirty and not be this fucking inconsequential party girl.*

Since Dale left, the only place she talked to her mother was at work, where she answered questions with a vague *hmmm,* insinuating there were important people buzzing about and she couldn't discuss her personal life. Veronica worked as a secretary in the sociology department at Columbia. She could walk to work, but she despised her job. And in the last year she'd noticed that the Birkenstock Brigade, the older, pristinely academic female professors were retiring and being replaced by young professors, women who seemed alarmingly like her, except probably they hadn't dropped out of Columbia during their first year of graduate school to follow a psychotic, married sculptor to London and lived there for nine confoundingly boring and dreamy months, surviving on Cadbury fruit and nut bars and sex.

She dropped the noodle cup on the floor and rolled over, grabbing Dale's pillowcase. It was smudged with make-up from nights he'd arrived home from playing too exhausted to wash his face. What agony to look at his smears of black eyeliner and iridescent bruise-purple eye shadow above a kiss of lipstick, just a cherry blob until Veronica held it close to her face and saw the feathered indentations of his chapped lips. She thought of Saint Veronica, who pressed a cool cloth to the face of Jesus when he collapsed under the cross to Calvary, a friend in deed, and the image of Jesus' face transferring to the cloth—Veronica's Veil—proving for all time how Saint Veronica stepped away from the hissing crowd to comfort her savior, how she chose love over conformity. Her mother had chosen Saint Veronica as a namesake because of her kindness to Jesus, and because she never endured the typical martyrdom of female saints. But to Veronica the name was a hex. She believed Saint Veronica suffered terribly after meeting Jesus, that she wandered the streets staring at the miracle of his face on the cloth, thinking: What now? What now?

Saint Veronica's veil was kept at Saint Peter's in Rome, where bastard scientists had declared it a fake; they claimed that carbon dating proved the veil didn't exist during the time of Christ. Veronica yanked the pillowcase off the pillow, the smell of Dale's sweat and his Kiehl's silk hair groom filling her throat, and mashed it into her laundry bag.

Maybe the face of Christ resisted carbon dating, maybe Saint Veronica burned the real veil in a fit of passion or pique, maybe Dale would come home tonight, rolling in late after she'd slept for a few hard hours and press his face to hers, whispering, hi, baby, as the moon slivered into the sun.

At 4:23 A.M. Veronica sat up in bed, blinking at the digital clock as if it might soothe her. Someone was in the kitchen. She'd dead bolted the door so she couldn't entertain the glorious hope that it was Dale standing repentently in the kitchen gulping down a glass of water before he begged for forgiveness. The security gate on the kitchen window was a knick-knack that had never worked. She owned no weapons and had never taken a self-defense course, believing if she knew how to defend herself she would be attacked. Fear came as the sensation of dry ice steaming her lungs. Was it payback time? All the decisions she'd ever made—not to marry Barry Brown, who slept soundly, she imagined, tucked up against his wife in an opulent, tacky house in the suburbs; reading "The Road Less Traveled" during her valedictory speech in high school while silently dedicating it to herself—all those self-congratulatory moments wailed into the frenetic drumming of her heart, her siren song of regret.

She jammed her hand in her mouth to keep her teeth from chattering like a wind-up skeleton and prayed: God, if you help me I will attend mass weekly; I will stop offering homeless people a confused smile when they ask for money; I will love all people as you have loved us, and I will stop wasting your time and mine praying for goddamn Dale to come back to me.

Veronica closed her eyes and projected herself into a happy future: a narrow hospital bed, where a nurse had just slumped a baby on Veronica's stomach, a tiny baby, still bluish, still attached to Veronica by a length of ropy umbilical cord. The feeling that she was tethered to a Martian subsided into swells of aching, dreamy love as the baby peered up at her.

The books say you should hide in your apartment and wait for an intruder to leave, but the vision of the baby gave her courage. She crept out of bed, flinching as the floor boards creaked, and slunk along the dark hallway and into the kitchen. She made the sign of the cross and flipped the switch.

A brown rat with a glue pad attached to its back lurched around in the overturned trash, the maze of coffee filters and gummy rice and napkins and brownie crumbs. She'd purchased the rodent glue strips when Dale moved out, believing herself too much of a sissy to actually pull back the metal latch on a wooden trap and flip an animal into the trash. But this was worse. She grabbed the broom and chased the rat into the hallway, swatting him, terrified he would turn around and tear into her bare ankle and infect her with a new strain of the Bubonic plague, her hands sweating so much she could hardly hold the broom, could hardly click on the lamp in the living room. The rat tried to dart under the couch, but Veronica smacked it, getting it back on track toward the door where it seemed to know to wait patiently while Veronica unlocked the four locks.

"Get out, out, out," she cried, flinging open the door, wondering if the poor rat could eventually wiggle out of the trap.

The rat scurried out, swaybacked. Veronica looked closer and saw a dull penny stuck to the glue trap, and one of Dale's curly black hairs—Mother of God, a pubic hair?

She locked up and drank the last few ounces of Dale's vodka.

She thought to open *How To Get Married In One Year Or Less* and inscribe it: *Dear Betty, Congratulations! You did it, girl, in less than a year!* This way, it looked like a bachelorette party gift; if she was killed later in the night, no condescending homicide detective could type up a humiliating report: *A single woman murdered in her apartment, she dreamed of marriage and had purchased an instructional book.*

Sunny Sunday morning, the first real spring day, the stabbing fact of Dale's absence dulled by the bliss of another day off work. Veronica tore around the apartment gathering up her dirty laundry and clothes Dale left behind—heavily pilled tube socks, soft jeans, and a T-shirt with "Haley's Glamorama" embossed across the chest in sparkly rainbow letters. She would wash his smelly clothes before packing them away in the Lane Cedar chest by her bed, her loss-of-hope chest. She walked to the Laundromat on 100th and Central Park West with her big black laundry bag bobbing over her shoulder, Mrs. Claus slogging through the chores while Santa cavorted with a new elf.

Posters of women in lingerie holding machetes and assault rifles covered the Laundromat's walls. The owner, a tall, silent red-haired woman who collected lint, sat behind the counter reading Penthouse and scribbling notes in a spiral. How Veronica and Dale had laughed at the way she race-walked over when she heard their dryer buzz, flagging them out of the way as she lunged for the lint trap. Oh, everything had been such a lark then, other people's loneliness—ha, ha, ha! Veronica inserted her quarters and sorted colors, tossing her clothes in with Dale's, dumping in detergent. What an ass she'd been to save his clothes, to sniff after them like a bloodhound.

She reached down in her bag for the final item, Dale's stained pillow case, which she plunged in the water, immersing her hand with regret and shivering terror, an archeologist gone mad, chucking dinosaur bones down the garbage disposal, unraveling mummies for sport, all evidence of their shared life swirling through the sudsy water.

And then a family of four walked in, the parents haggard and snapping, carrying old plastic clothes baskets, the children—a girl and a boy, Veronica guessed seven and five—dazzling in jeans and backpacks and crazy morning hair. The parents argued their way back to the gray industrial-sized machines and the children sat down on a bench across from Veronica. As the girl took a pad of paper out of her backpack, her markers fell out and rolled across the floor. Veronica gathered up the markers—the scented kind: watermelon pink, licorice black, forest green—and handed them back to the girl.

"Thank you, Ma'am," the girl said, pressing her chin to her chest.

Ma'am, thought Veronica. *My God*. How she mourned for *Miss*.

The parents slapped baggies of quarters on top of the machines and started up the washers. But the father had stuck a shirt in the wrong load. The mother ordered him back from the machine as she pulled dark, wet clothes out like seaweed, screeching, "Christ, it must have sunk to the bottom like a goddamn rock." And the father crossed his arms over his chest, pouting, a far away look in his eyes, as if mourning those lives he might have chosen—pilot, rock star, international banker. Both parents were oblivious of their children, who hummed loudly as they drew fanciful dinosaurs on their notepads. To anyone walking in the Laundromat, it would appear that Veronica was the mother, that these children were hers, and in her purse she carried graham crackers, band-aids, sugarless gum and Kleenex, instead of a journal and eyeliner and loose aspirin tablets, and she was busy, busy, busy. Certainly she had no time to loll around mourning an aging glam-rocker. The kids kept her so damn busy!

And wouldn't her children want to know about the life she'd had before they were born? Veronica loved sorting through her own mother's single-girl relics: the goofy sonnets from Danny Van Buskirk, the sapphire-chip earrings from doomed Kevin Martin. She opened her washer and fished through the wet laundry until she found the pillow case. Soap bubbles sparkled the worn cotton, but Dale's smudgy eyes and lips remained. She wrung out the pillow case and jammed it in her coat pocket, thinking, *Oh, Dale,* wondering if fate and her own idiocy would doom her to a life at the Laundromat. Veronica: an old lady in crepe-soled orthopedic shoes and a ratty house dress staring at circles of moisture on the dryer door, her hands slow and tremulous, her face pruney, her heart still stupid and wild.

She grabbed her purse and bolted out of the Laundromat, raising her hand to a cab that barreled across two lanes of traffic to pick her up. And then, everywhere, omens. The sun pierced a cloud shaped like a buoyant infant lying on her back; the cab driver displayed a baby picture in a heart-shaped frame on the dashboard. And the Upper West Side jangled with church bells and squirrels, babies and dogs and husbands and wives—a warm, beckoning universe—so Veronica overtipped her cab driver for luck and rushed into Oh! Baby! the shop where she'd purchased the coat for Gina's baby. The one crocheted coat remaining was trimmed with spring-green ribbon, a strand of grass swirling through milk.

The saleswoman rung up the coat and wrapped it in layers of green paper. She handed it to Veronica in a shopping bag patterned with fat babies—a seventy eight dollar package— lots of lunches at Mama Joy's deli, but more importantly, an investment in the future. As Veronica glided out the door on a saccharine shopping high, she looked in the mirrored windows of Oh! Baby! Wrinkles showed around her lips and eyes, a series of arrows pointing to her exit from babedom.

How odd it was, she thought, to still think of herself as a prize, a hidden treasure really, after all the years of failures and screw-ups; it was probably a delusion bordering on a true mental illness that would require hospitalization. It had been a long time since she'd arrived in Manhattan in the mid-eighties, just another stocky Holly Go-Lightly in Doc Martens, another 22 year old midwestern novelty act. She crossed the street praying it wasn't too late, praying that someone would love and marry her and be a good father to their children, then chastising herself for how grotesquely wimpy and uncool it sounded—show me the mini-van, show *me* the mini-van—and as she stepped up onto the pavement she looked into the amazed eyes of Dale, who held hands with a pale blonde girl. A pale blonde girl wearing the leather jacket she'd bought Dale for Christmas three years back.

"Veronica," he said, softly, with shocked sorrow, as if gasping, "cancer."

Here was fierce coincidence, fresh, impressive torture on a Sunday morning, the old story-*Out of all the boys in New York City*—her very own Pontius Pilate waiting to cross 84th street. Her thoughts shuffled, zooming randomly: On their first date, inside the penguin house in Central Park, he'd said, "Veronica, a beautiful name for beautiful you," and kaboom!—Manhattan was hers; last summer he'd held her hand as she looked into her grandmother's open casket and said, "She still smells like her watery old basement," and he said, "Maybe her dress was down there," and it was so good to have a partner to help navigate the shitty waters of adulthood. Now he held Whiskey Jenny's hand while she stared into the traffic with studied dimness, while hurt and horror and humiliation seized Veronica's heart, while she rued not wearing her black boots with three inch heels, where she saw a steeple towering in her peripheral vision and thought *God is such a total bastard*, simultaneously thinking that such thoughts should be saved for car crashes and terminal diagnoses, that seeing her old boyfriend with someone else didn't warrant a fresh bout of atheism. Her old boyfriend! Well, it certainly had a jolly, junior-high ring to it, but her hands trembled, rattling the shopping bag against her leg.

"This is kind of terrible," Dale said. He dropped Whiskey Jenny's hand and gave his forehead the three stooges slap, mumbling dramatically: "Veronica, this is—"

"—Whiskey Jenny," Veronica said, taking in the girl's cat-gray eyes, sandalwood perfume, perfect teeth—crowns?—and confident little grin.

"It's Jenny," she said crisply. "Whiskey Jenny is my stage name."

"Is that right?" Veronica said. "Your stage name?" It was hard to smile condescendingly with intense nausea rising from her stomach to her chest, the sensation she might projectile vomit her heart onto the sidewalk, a flapping red steak for the next dog to eat.

"So, how've you been, Veronica?" The false falsetto of Dale's voice comforted her—perhaps a cruel race of aliens had brainwashed him to fall in love with this recovering alcoholic spoken word performer—but then he squished closer to Whiskey Jenny so people would stop brushing between the two of them. Jesus, he could pass for her father; Dale turned 40 in two weeks and Whiskey Jenny looked 22, maybe 23. Why did men not know that a younger woman made them look older? And how sad that he'd officially joined the generic world of men, Dale, who had been hers.

"I'm fine," Veronica said. She put her hand in her pocket and touched his wet pillow case.

"Well, it was great meeting you, Veronica," Whiskey Jenny said, extending her hand as if they were about to shake on a business deal.

Veronica envisioned the conversation that would take place in 30 seconds: *Oh my God, I feel so terrible. She looks so lonely. I'm such a horrible person; No, Dale, it's not your fault. We just fell in love. She needs to take responsibility for her own life.*

And then they would go home and have sex.

She squeezed her hand around the pillow case, thrust it out of her pocket and placed it in Whiskey Jenny's open hand.

Then Veronica stepped back, enjoying this sudden pshychobitch drama of her own creation—Dale moaning, "Christ almighty;" Whiskey Jenny's corporate smile wavering into a grimace of confusion as she unfurled the wet pillow case—and she turned away, resisted the urge to look back, and began the long walk to the Laundromat, where she would transfer her clothes to the dryer and Dale's clothes to the trash before taking the tiny coat out of the shopping bag and pressing it to her face. The crocheted cotton swaddled her skin as she day-dreamed about her baby. She prayed that the coat was more than a soft icon, imagining Emma or Pauline, Mathew or Jack: *how I've loved you, how I've dreamed of you.*

I Fly Unto You

At the Feast of the Assumption Mass, a panel of sunlight shone through a row of stained-glass windows, flashing through the rich reds and purples of the saints' robes, before pouring onto the pale gold of the Virgin Mary's arm, and settling on a teenage girl sitting cross-legged in the front pew, distracting Father Jack Gothers from his homily about the human goodness of Mary.

The parishioners at Our Lady of Victory stopped gazing at Father Jack with faces so dazed and complacent that they seemed to meld together, featureless and pale as a communion wafer. Instead, everyone looked at the light, then bobbed their heads around, stealing a side view of the girl who stared up at the sprays of pink gladioli on the altar. Her hair hung in loose auburn waves past her shoulders, and she wore a white sleeveless dress and combat boots. In her right hand she clutched a missalette. The golden light radiated from her body, bouncing up towards the window, then falling back, engulfing her again. To Father Jack, she looked like a triumphant young saint— beautiful Lucy illumined by flaming lanterns. The image was slightly ruined by the girl's knee-high boots, until Father Jack remembered—not gentle Saint Lucy, Saint Joan of Arc! She was Joan of Arc, headed to the trenches in her big boots and paneled in the strongest battle-armor: God's golden light.

The girl raised her hand from her lap and looked at the statue of the Virgin Mary next to the altar. Mary's left hand was cupped in a weary half-wave; her right hand supported the bottom of baby Jesus, whom she cradled in the crook of her arm. Since baby Jesus' marble head was roughly the same size as Mary's, the King of Kings looked like a dwarf swaddled in blue blankets. The girl moved her lips silently while she raised her hand higher, tilting her wrist and curling her fingers into the same crippled wave as the Virgin's.

Specks of dust floated in the beam of light, which lost it's golden hue as it widened and enveloped the first pew, then the second and the third, flooding through the stained glass windows, until the whole church filled with the palest kaleidoscope of light.

"Imagine the Virgin Mother's joy when she discovered she'd been chosen to bear the son of God," Father Jack said, continuing. "But let's also imagine her courage and the strength of her faith. We usually think of Mary as a young woman in her twenties, but when the archangel Gabriel visited Mary, she was still a young girl. Joseph was forty years old, but Biblical scholars have figured Mary to be no more than fifteen. Fifteen! A teenage mother. Imagine her not in a hooded blue robe, but in a plaid school uniform, bulging at the waist. Imagine her courage!"

Parishioners touched their fingers to their necks as they stared at the Virgin Mary holding her jumbo baby. Father Jack knew that worshippers at Our Lady of Victory in Newton, Kansas didn't enjoy a controversial homily. They'd grown accustomed to the good humor of Bill Fitzsimmons, the previous, beloved priest from Our Lady who was at the hospice in Wichita dying of colon cancer. Father Jack had served as parish priest for just three weeks, so he'd only met the activist parishioners: the darling ladies of the rosary society who also ran the free lunch program, the strange couple who served as youth ministers, the truly friendly, and the kiss-ups who liked to include the parish priest on their social roster.

The sun shifted again, muting the light further, and the church grew shaded and somber. Father Jack attempted a soothing wrap-up. "Let us all try to emulate Mary's devotion to God, her faith, and her love for her son, our Lord Jesus Christ." He walked over to the red velvet chair—the throne—where he sat in silent reflection before continuing the liturgy.

Relieved from his holy day duties, Father Jack escaped to his new house, the three bedroom rectory featuring a sunken living room and wall-to-wall pine-green carpeting. In the kitchen he grabbed a bottle of Budweiser from the fridge, where he found an unfamiliar Corning Ware dish on the bottom shelf. Stuck to the lid was a Post-it note that read: Enjoy! The woman hired by the parish to cook and clean for him had her own key, and liked to prepare homey casseroles. He lifted the lid a crack and smelled brown sugar and mustard. Good God, was it Beanie Weenies?

He slugged down the beer standing up. He hated the trendy green kitchen and all the ultra-modern appliances. But the cornucopia of dried wild flowers he'd bought at Our Lady's Saturday bazaar looked cheery hanging above the kitchen sink. He smiled, remembering the loaded look the maiden Renneker sisters exchanged as he'd mulled over the flowers.

He missed the rectory at his previous parish in Davenport, the stone house built at the turn of the century, but recently remodeled, so you could pace in the drafty rooms and feel holy and poetic, but also cool down in the a/c or pop a frozen burrito in the microwave situated in a specially-made oak coffin over the cast iron stove. He missed the Chesterfield sofa in front of the bay window, where Mr. Pibb, the elderly cat, sat on a worn velvet pillow watching swallows dip in the bird bath. He missed his organic vegetable patch and the perennial garden where he'd cultivated ivory daffodils and ruby hollyhocks. The yard at his new house featured a bright, pesticide-green lawn and ornamental shrubs.

"Priests are often lonely on Sunday afternoon," Father David Pearson, his beloved homiletics professor, had once told Jack. And now he understood this to be true. In LaGrange he'd shared the house with the young, good-natured parochial vicar, and before that, in Coffeyville, he'd been the parochial vicar; he had never lived alone, never struggled with the ceaseless temptations of the unobserved. Father Pearson had also told a stunned class of first year seminary students, "Don't worry too much about masturbation. If you're going to be celibate, it's natural to assume you'll be bashing the Bishop from time to time."

He went to his bedroom, pulled the shade, and undressed. He clicked on the clock radio and lay down on his twin bed. On the radio, the Rolling Stones sang, "Take me down little Suzy, take me down." The bottom edge of the shade skimmed the window sill, which was sparkling white and free of the dead bugs, paint chips and the white-painted nails an old house gathers. The pull on the shade had a ring covered with white thread. He held it close to his face, starring at the layers of whiteness, then traced it over his lips, enjoying the textured softness, before letting it drop again.

The usual crew of hard-core sinners showed up for confession on Friday morning—the ladies of the rosary society. Mrs. Ellen Laehy stared at the flat, colorless diamonds in her wedding band and confessed to feeling jealous when her sister-in-law won two hundred dollars at Monday night's bingo. Father Jack leaned across the card table separating them, and asked if Ellen had punched her sister-in-law—did she give her good one?—when she'd heard her scream, "Bingo!"

Ellen threw her head back, choking out the brittle laugh of a heavy smoker, a sound that filled the airless room with the shadowed figures of women he'd loved: his mom and his Aunt

Gigi smoking and playing hearts at the kitchen table while smoke filled the house. "Just a couple of witches smoking our Salems," his mom would say; and Candy Nelson, his girlfriend from high school, with her burnished red hair and flour white skin. She smoked cigarettes ringed with bright flowers—Eve's, weren't they? Father Jack imagined a long-haired woman in the Garden of Eden: yeah, I'll take a bite of the damn apple, then I'll have me a smoke.

Though it seemed crazy to assign rote prayers to Ellen, when surely the Kingdom of Heaven was hers, she expected it. So, he told her to say a few Hail Mary's and Our Father's. Then, with the official business completed, Ellen pulled a foil-wrapped pan from her canvas bag. "Just some of my cinnamon rolls, Father."

Cinnamon Rolls! What good people there were in the world. He'd dined at China Garden the previous night and his fortune cookie read, "It is no small feat to improve the quality of the day"—a slogan many of the women at Our Lady had written over their hearts. He smiled at Ellen, taking in her aging beauty: the mosaic of broken blood vessels, her silver hair pulled into a twist, the too-sweet smell of flowery perfume.

On her way out, she called over her shoulder, "Just one more, Father, then you can be home to your lunch."

Then the girl who had been shrouded in sunlight at Mass walked in, half-grinning and half-smirking, and slung her purple suede backpack on the floor.

"I'm Abby Crilly," she said. "Hello Father Jack."

"Hello Abby," He held out his hand to the Samsonite folding chair opposite him.

She sat down and inhaled deeply. "Forgive me Father, for I have sinned. It has been, oh, wow, I guess about six months since my last confession. Partially because of me, but partially I felt, why add to Father Fitzsimmons work load when he already has cancer?"

"Very understandable."

He tried to concentrate on her face while skimming the names of the rock groups on her Lollapalooza T-shirt. He recognized none, confirming his fears that he was old at forty-two. Her clogs clattered against the hardwood floor as she crossed her legs. Father Jack peered beneath the table, and noticed the surprising bands of mint-green daisies showing on the inch of skin between the cuff of her jeans and her clogs. Damn! Had she seen him looking? He longed for the days of the grand confessionals, those carved mahogany sanctuaries where parishioner and priest sat on either side of a dark screen. Anonymity would make it easier for those confessing troubling sins, and he wouldn't need to feign looks of concern about overdue library books or profanity.

"Go ahead," Father Jack told Abby.

"I have had sex outside of marriage, which has resulted in an unplanned pregnancy. I mean, I'm pregnant." Abby danced her fingers on the card table and grinned.

Her grin was so appealing that he grinned back at her, then bit down on his bottom lip and said soberly, " I see."

"For real?" She stood and held up the bottom of her T-shirt, exposing her flat stomach. An amethyst strung on a silver hoop pierced her navel.

"No, no, no. I mean *I see*, as in I understand what it is you're telling me. Not"—He held his fingertips to his eyes then pulled them quickly away—"I see."

She pulled her T-shirt down. "Oh God! I'm nervous. I'm not a total idiot, really. It's just that I'm in the fourth month, and that's when the books say you start to show. The baby's head is crowning over my hips."

He imagined a tiny baby floating in her womb—her womb?—wearing a jeweled, golden crown.

"Have you informed the baby's father of this?"

"Sort of." She shrugged and sat down.

"And may I ask what his reaction was?"

"He seemed pretty surprised. I guess we fell into the one percentile that the pills don't work for. Which I guess I shouldn't have been using in the first place. Or whatever."

"Have you told your parents?"

"No. No way."

"Do you think they'd react . . . "

"They'd die. On the spot. Plus, they think I'm off to Notre Dame next week. Dad's alma mater. I did sort of want to go, I visited in April and it seemed nice, though, you know, kind of like a Disneyland for Catholics?"

Father Jack smiled at her. Outside, the trash truck groaned through the alley.

Abby clapped her hands together and said, "Oh, I have a joke for you. I usually hate jokes, because there's all this weird pressure to laugh and then there's a ton of different ways to end up feeling embarrassed. And plus there's the problem of the person taking the joke the wrong way." She pressed her lips together, leaving a sparkling red trail on her front teeth. "Saint Paul dies and goes to heaven. He gets to hang out with all the angels and the saints, but the person he's dying to meet is Mary, because he has this important question for her. There's a long line of people waiting to meet her, because she's the sentimental favorite, of course. When he finally meets her, Paul says, 'Mary, in all the pictures I've ever seen of you, you're always holding the baby Jesus and looking oh, so very sad. As the holy woman chosen to give birth to the King of Kings, why did you look so full of sorrow?' Mary shrugged and said, 'I wanted a girl.'"

He'd heard the joke at umpteen Christmas parties, but Father Jack laughed, and seeing that his laughter relaxed Abby, he laughed again, and the air conditioner kicked in, ruffling the foil on the pan of rolls and flooding the small room with sugary coldness, and she laughed with him, just a bit, creasing the dimples around her mouth, and he let out great whoops and ho-ho-hos, and even to himself he sounded crazy, frantic as last year's Salvation Army Santa, later revealed as a crystal meth user.

"Man!" he finally said, "that was a good one, Abby."

"Thanks. I'm glad you didn't take it the wrong way. You know, my family's gone to Our Lady of Victory for five generations now. My Grandma Eileen believed that if you held your hand in the same position of the Mary on the altar, while saying the Memorare, you could commune with the Virgin Mother who would intercede for all your prayers."

Abby raised her hand stiffly, imitating the statue's fey wave, and said, "O most gracious Virgin Mary, never was it known that anyone who fled to your protection, implored your help, or sought your intercession was left unaided. Inspired by this confidence, I fly unto you, O virgin of virgins, my mother. Etcetera, etcetera."

She flexed her fingers before lowering her hand. "I am *through* with petitions. Now I offer prayers of thanks to the Virgin Mary, because I'm, at least temporarily, but hopefully forever, cured of rheumatoid arthritis.

Her face reddened, and she spoke with the urgency of a lonely person, though Father Jack couldn't imagine Abby being lonely.

"My hands used to be so stiff in the morning! Just like the statue of the Blessed Virgin, only both my hands were crippled. I wondered if God was sending me some sort of sign, through my illness, because every night I prayed that I would feel better in the morning, yet I always woke wondering if I was getting backlogged into a huge vault of unanswered prayers and crawled out of bed like I was ninety-five years old because everything hurt so bad. This all started when I was a sophomore. My feet swelled up so much that I couldn't wear my favorite shoes, it was goodbye platforms , hello Birkenstock sandals." She cleared her throat. "Which I realize is sort of a shallow thing to be upset about. But now my joints are fine—they're perfect!"

"Abby. Gee." A soaring, wired hopefulness closed his throat. "I didn't even know a young person could get arthritis. So, you feel better pregnant?"

"RA goes into remission when you're pregnant. I want to have a baby every year! I'll be the little old lady who loved in the shoe, who had so many children she didn't know what to do!"

"Sounds great!" Then he added, "Well, if that's what you want, when you're older. And when your have your education. And when you're married of course."

"I'm kidding about the shoe and all the kids. I can tell you the truth, right? Because people can tell you that they've murdered a whole town or whatever, and you're not allowed to tell anyone because it's a special priestly law? Secrecy is sacred, right?"

During the offertory hymn at the following Sunday's mass, Father Jack surveyed the church and found the Crilly family standing with the other late-comers at the back of the church. He pitied Abby's parents, who had no idea their oldest daughter was not destined for South Bend, but taking the Amtrak to Chicago on Monday morning. Abby planned to live in a friend's studio apartment and clerk at a record store. The baby would be born in December, and Abby would come home for a visit. Her parents, over the initial shock and buoyed by holiday cheer, would delight in spending Christmas with their first grand baby. In January she would start college in Chicago, paying for her fees and day care with money saved from her record store wages.

Father Jack admired Abby's careful planning, but he mostly felt alarmed. She wanted to breast feed, she told him, and if she had problems breastfeeding, she would switch to soy milk instead of using regular formula; did he know that cow's milk was pure poison? She planned to buy basic black maternity clothes so she could wear them as over-sized separates after the baby was born. She was going to subscribe to *hip mama* magazine.

An elderly usher brought the collection basket to the altar. He wore a cream and tan knit bowling shirt, a replica of one Father Jack's dad had often worn with old-man Sansabelt pants. His parents had died of heart attacks within six months of each other, orphaning him at thirty-nine. He glanced back at Abby, who had her hand raised towards the Virgin Mary. With her wit, beauty and fervent prayers, she epitomized the child he would have wanted, his long lost dream daughter. The next pope might let priests marry, but it would be too late for him.

The usher placed the collection basket in Father Jack's hands. Father Jack blessed the basket of money and prayed for peace; he prayed not to be a fickle, middle-aged lover of Christ.

Coins jingled, and there was the soft shuffling of folded bills and collection envelopes as Father Jack raised the offering over his head.

"We Pray, Lord," he said, "that our sacrifice will be acceptable to you."

That night the phone rang just as Father Jack had fallen asleep, but like most priests, he'd learned to answer late night calls gracefully.

"Father Jack?

He recognized her voice, but briskly said, "Yes, yes. Who's calling please?"

"It's me," she whispered. "I mean, Abby. Abby Crilly. I'm sorry to call so late, but I want to tell you something. You know how I told you that I fell into the one percentile who got pregnant when they were taking the pill?"

"I remember," he whispered.

"I was lying. It was a big lie. Um, should I be telling you this over the phone?"

"I don't see any reason why you shouldn't. The phone is just fine" he whispered. But then he felt shamed to be reclining in bed and speaking in a soft, excited voice in the dark. He sat up and clicked on the lamp.

"Oh, the phone is great," she said breathlessly. "I sometimes wish my hand were a phone, that I had the number pad glued to my palm, that's how much I love the telephone. Anyway. Did I wake you up?"

"No, no. Please."

"Well, as I said, I lied about using the pill because I didn't need to use the pill, because I'm not sexually active, I've never had sex with anyone." She paused, then said, as if reading from a textbook, "there's no biological explanation for my pregnancy."

"Oh, Alrighty," he said dumbly. "Are you sure about that?"

Mother of God. Had she been raped? Could she be having a psychotic break? It happened occasionally with pregnant girls so deeply in denial they claimed an immaculate conception. Jesus! How could he have read things so wrong? He'd never questioned her emotional stability.

"Yes, I'm quite positive."

"Listen," he said. "What should I do to help you?"

"No, no there's nothing. I just wanted to tell you, that's all. I know there's no way you can believe me, but that's okay. Because I feel so wonderful without the arthritis. You know the song, 'Lord you take away the sins of the world, have mercy on us?' Sometimes in church I would sing, 'Lord, you take away the sins of the world, won't you, take away, my auto-immune disease?' It made my sisters laugh. Well, I'm off to Chicago tomorrow. So. Bye."

"Abby, wait," he said, then heard the phone line buzz.

He clicked off the lamp. Outside, a car hummed down the dark street, and as the headlights cut a stream of golden light through his dark bedroom, he remembered the light that engulfed Abby at the Feast of the Assumption mass. Could that have been some sort of . . . sign? He closed his eyes. Good God. Like everyone else, he was foregoing the Mysteries of faith, wanting clues and arrows, a hologram and a compass. Soon he would start burning cones of patchouli incense and rubbing crystals for inner harmony. But poor Abby! She must be ill, or why would she need to tell such a lie? Lots of teenage girls got pregnant and kept their babies without scandal. He dozed off thinking of Abby, then dreamed they were kissing, though the dream felt light and spacy, shrouded in gossamer. A giant disco ball appeared above their heads, dusting opalescent light on Abby's face, and she floated out of his arms and started to dance. As she swiveled her hips and gently flipped her wrists, she whispered, "Look how I can move now."

He woke disappointed that the dream hadn't progressed, and disappointed in himself. It was vaguely smutty, he figured, to have lustful thoughts about a woman, but disgusting to fantasize about a young pregnant girl. Damn! Why had he dreamed that, he wondered, when what he wanted to do was to go to the bus station and give her a hug, then pull his wallet from his back pocket—the universal gesture of fathers everywhere—and hand her a couple of twenties. Abby was virtually a child. But then there was the fullness of her mouth, the sweep of her hair. Jesus Christ! Well, that was that, a done deal, he'd turned into a pervert, a perverted priest—Father Jack-off—he would start ogling the counter girls at Burger King, then progress to installing two-way mirrors in the women's bathroom at Our Lady of Victory.

He set the alarm clock for eight o'clock since the only Chicago-bound train left at nine—he'd checked—and tried to sleep.

He'd envisioned the train station as a brick building that opened onto a wooden platform where people sipped from Styrofoam cups of steaming coffee as their good dress shoes click-clicked along the oak planks. But the station, housed in a vinyl-sided pole building, led to a concrete platform painted swimming pool blue. Inside, a frazzled ticket agent sat enclosed in a gated plastic bubble. People slept or read the newspaper on orange plastic chairs connected by metal bars. Father Jack strolled through the station with what he hoped was great casualness. He wore chinos and a blue shirt, but street clothes were never enough for a priest. You needed a mask to go incognito; you needed plastic surgery. Through the smudged glass doors that led to the platform, he saw Abby swinging a green suitcase back and forth. He mopped his face with his handkerchief, blaming his lust on the succulent Kansas summer. He wished it were winter, Christ's season, and that snow drifted on the platform, and that the air smelled of pine and holly; he wished Abby wore a sensible coat, maybe a cheerful red coat, with kidskin gloves and warm boots instead of the black slip dress that fell to her hips, and high-heeled sandals.

He would walk out and say good-bye, but first he needed to do a quick parishioner-check. As he surveyed the line stretching past the ticket bubble, he saw a teenage girl with bad acne and stringy blonde hair approaching the people in line. She held a wicker basket of pastel paper rosebuds fastened to green pipe cleaner stems. As she tried to hand out her flowers, each person averted their eyes. The girl scanned the crowd, sighing, then walked directly to Father Jack.

"Jesus wants you to fill your heart with love," she said wearily, holding out a pale blue rose.

Father Jack remembered standing in line, years ago, at the old Bishop's cafeteria with two friends from seminary. Another homely girl had pressed a paper flower in his hand and said, "Choose Jesus."

One of his young friends whispered, I believe he already has.

He had looked at the girl, then back at the chalk board listing the daily specials and drummed his fingers on his chin before he gaily said, "I think I'll choose ham on marbled rye instead." How pleased he had been with this retort, how smugly he and the other boys had laughed, while the girl, accustomed to mockery, simply turned and approached the next person in the lunch line.

Now he accepted the paper rose and this girl said, "Jesus saves souls."

He thanked her, opened his wallet and handed her a ten dollar bill. The girl folded the money and stuck it down the front of her dress. She lifted her face to his, then placed her hand under his chin. She stepped closer, brushing her rough lips against his ear.

"Jesus saves souls," she whispered, "and redeems them for cash and valuable prizes." The girl flicked her tongue into his ear, then dashed through the bus station.

Father Jack cleared his throat excessively, as if preparing for a long homily. As a warm bead of saliva rolled luxuriously into his ear canal, he looked at the doors of the platform and saw Abby waving and motioning for him to come outside. He walked over and flung open the door, then ran to her, and in the brief, otherworldly seconds before he realized his foolishness, he'd dropped the flower and picked Abby up by her waist.

"That was so cool," she said, as he put her gently down. "I'm trying to remember this moment, even though I just lived it. Do you ever do that?"

Father Jack searched the platform, and saw an elderly couple frowning at him. Did they go to our Lady of Victory? He flashed them a smile as they looked away.

"I'm sorry, Abby," he whispered. "I shouldn't have done that."

"Oh no!" She skimmed her hand across her stomach "Don't be sorry. The doctor at Planned Parenthood said I could do low-impact aerobics up until my sixth month. Physical activity doesn't harm the baby."

"What I meant is, I'm a priest." But the words sounded so shameful and cinematic that he stared down at the graffiti carved in the concrete: Carla loves John, You Suck, God loves you.

"I know you're a priest," Abby said.

"I'm sorry, I'm just disoriented. There was this really strange girl in the terminal."

Abby nodded. "That's the crazy girl. I saw her in there with you. She has fourteen different personalities. She was on Jerry Springer."

"Oh, great," Father Jack said. "She's mentally ill *and* exploited."

"Well, it was a pretty interesting show." She unzipped her purse and pulled out a newspaper clipping. "Behold," she said. The sunlight caught the sparkles in her purple eye shadow. "I show you a miracle."

She handed him the clipping, and as he read about the clinical studies for a new rheumatoid arthritis medicine, Abby stiffened her hand into the Virgin's wave and whispered the Memorare: "Oh blessed Virgin Mary, never has it been known that anyone who sought your blessing was left unaided. Inspired by this confidence, I fly unto you."

Abby had underlined the last passage of the article with red ink, and scribbled hearts and flowers in the margin: *The new active substance is designed to interact with the immune system, inhibiting inflammation of and damage to the joints without weakening the body's defense against infections. It will be available all around the world in two years time.*

As he lifted his eyes from the page, Abby said, "It worked, my prayers worked. In two years I'll be chasing a toddler instead of hobbling after him, or her." She wiggled her fingers. "Look at this flexibility. I could play the piano! I could chop fire wood."

"In Chicago?"

Over the crackling PA, the ticket agent announced the train was approaching.

"I know you don't believe me, " Abby said, "about the baby being another miracle But it's true. It is!" With her hand on her hip, she whispered comically, "It's not like the world doesn't need another savior." She seemed close to tears.

He reached out to touch her shoulder, but she grabbed his hand and gripped it so tightly he felt her fingernails pinching half-moons into his palm.

"I have a song for you," she said. "But if you get the joke, which is not actually a joke at all, you'll see that it's a song *you* should sing to me." She took a deep breath and sang, softly, "If I were a carpenter and you were a lady, would you marry me anyway, would you have my baby?" She paused, as if trying to remember the words, and hung her head exhaustedly.

Father Jack felt the song inside of him, the sweet, corny spell vibrating his brain. He gazed at Abby's shining hair, at the rhinestone barrette holding her coiled hair, and then at the soft map of her bare neck: the golden clasp of her necklace, and a raised, pre-cancerous strawberry mole he wished to cover with cream sun block. He started to imagine the two of them walking through a brush of falling leaves in Lincoln Park, and touring the aquarium hand-in-hand. He wanted the angel of God to whisper, "Fear not," as he dozed next to Abby in a King-sized bed at the Surf hotel. He thought of his closet of cassocks, the half-finished bottle of Rogaine and the Playboy stashed in his medicine closet, his new Honda in the parking lot: cotton, chemicals, glass, paper, metal. How sad, how paltry, an object seemed compared to a human being! And how sad even was the spirit, the soul—Jesus himself—compared to skin, hair, the pressure of fingers, a banging heart.

Abby raised her head. "Mostly I want one person to believe me, just one. "

Then the crazy girl appeared behind the smudged glass doors. She traced a swollen, lop-sided heart in the grime and waved goodbye.

Father Jack had wanted something else: A flock of geese to appear unseasonably and in the wrong formation, as a crucifix beating across the sky, the face of the Virgin sketched in the diaphanous clouds. He wanted the platform shadowed in gloomy cloud-cover, while the sun funneled one bright, celestial ray on Abby. But as he looked at the curve of Abby's breasts beneath her thin dress, he felt his heart open to the idea of her immaculate conception, or at least to her own belief in the story. Faith, he thought, was only compassion for humans experiencing traumatic or glorious mysteries, for in believing their stories—tell me, oh, tell me again!—you might ease their loneliness, and your own.

No! He was being idiotic. But when he bowed his head, praying that God might give him the sudden grace to tell Abby goodbye, he noticed her ankles had swollen over the thin straps of her ankles, and he felt a crashing love for her that swallowed up God.

"I'll go with you to Chicago," Father Jack said quickly.

"Oh man, that rocks!" Abby threw her arms around him as a squawking voice announced the final boarding call to Chicago. Father Jack touched the moving muscles in her back. He pressed his face to her neck, breathing in the chemical bouquet of her hair, clinging to her, wanting to live in this first moment forever.

She whispered, "What should I call you?"

Saint Anne

My breasts ached with milk, hot as molten lava, heavy as brick. With my shirt dangling around my neck and the flaps of my nursing bra down, I stood in front of the toilet and tried out my breast pump. Through the hinges of the stall I saw a student primping in front of the mirror, painting her lips with a peachy gloss the color of Isabella's skin. Menthol cigarette smoke wafted over my head, a minted cloud of doom, then came an explosive crescendo from the next stall, followed by the deepest, relieved sigh.

I pulled the trigger of my hand-held pump again and again, stretching my nipple into a skinny purple arrow. Not one drop squeezed out. The brochure said that if you thought about your baby and relaxed, four ounces of milk would flow from each breast. But when I thought about Isabella—her chickeny 12-week old self adjusting to the world, flashing a worried, gummy smile, raising her bony starfish hands to me—my own hands trembled so I could hardly hold the pump, and my heart beat with the wings of a coked-up bird about to burst from my chest, shattering my breast bone, soaring away. Earlier that morning I'd plunged Isabella into a new world. I'd left her with Sherry Kinnersley, who seemed the least trashy of the low-cost daycare providers I'd interviewed, but who could have very well been psychotic. Day care: the Hellish, custodial ring of those two short words. How sad it was to leave Isabella at Sherry Kinnersley's house with a canister of powdered formula that looked like malt mix or Pixie Stick dust. Did my baby feel bewildered all over again, a newborn again, pushed from one womb to another?

Frantic, I switched breasts; I didn't want Isabella to drink formula at day care the next day, but pumping with my left hand was worse. I pulled the trigger too hard and lavender-black bruises blossomed on my areola, beneath the furious mouth of the suction cup. No milk. I stuck the pump in my back pack and hauled myself and my cannon ball breasts back to the Humanities office, where I worked as a secretary.

But wasn't everyone thrilled to see me on my first day back from maternity leave! Diane, the main secretary, gave me a bouquet of balloons that spelled out WELCOME BACK in puffy, rainbow letters. She asked too few questions about Isabella and didn't rave adequately about her baby picture before arguing passionately against a new rule issued by the by registrar's office, wherein students would now be identified by a seven, not a six digit identification number. I listened to her soliloquy, confused. I'd taken the job two months pregnant, for the health insurance, but she seemed to have daydreamed me into someone who cared. I'd forgotten about her yellow hair and yellow teeth, and the yellow plastered walls of the office, forgotten the rubber bands, the binders and Scotch tape and soft pink erasers; What did one do with such things? In my twelve weeks at home learning to care for Isabella, the rest of the world had melted away, an inconsequential ice age, leaving behind only new-world necessities: the pediatrician's office, the grocery store, the park, the Baby Gap.

"The temp was some religious nutso, dumb as a duck," Diane said, handing me a sheath of labels to type. "She left me buried in work. I'm going to need you to be on the ball even though you miss that baby like the devil."

"I didn't know how hard it would be to leave her," I whispered, my words the refrain from some hillbilly song, but how could I ever explain my craven desperation, equal only to the fullness of my heart when I looked at Isabella?

"You'll get used to it, sweetie," she said. "Everyone does."

I switched on the computer. Though my fingers remembered the keyboard, the letters swirled trickily: the k turned into half of Isabella's body, her right arm and leg splayed out; the x cartwheeled into a star, the silver star on her red sleeper, the s contained the curl of her teeny fingers that I straightened with kisses to her knuckles. Asthmatic with worry, I dialed Sherry Kinnersley's number. She said, *you again*, and *Isabella's fine; she took the bottle of formula fine; see you at five thirty, bye now.*

Was that Isabella crying in the background? My breasts tingled, a scramble of needles and pins, and milk leaked through my bra and shirt. As I blotted the wet streaks with Kleenex, Diane cleared her throat and wagged her finger at the clock, meaning it was time for me to hop up and brew a fresh pot of coffee for the chair of the department, Ray Dobbs.

"Don't forget, his-nibs likes it extra-strong," she whispered, conspiratorially yet imperious, glad to have someone lower on the food chain.

I slogged over to the Mr. Coffee pot. Did mommy neurosurgeons and mommy film producers feel this raging despair at work? I believed they did not. I held my arms stiffly away from my body, tin woodsman-like, so they wouldn't brush against my breasts as I spooned coffee crystals into a paper filter and cursed myself for not practicing with the pump, for expecting some last-minute benevolence: lotto jackpot or an inheritance from one of the rich ladies I'd read to at the nursing home back when I was a civic-minded college student. I remembered Viola McGraw, whom I'd adored for her reverence of Emily Dickinson and all things Avon, but now my toxic thoughts formed the phrase: drop dead and pony up the dough. I poured bottled water into the coffee pot, thinking how Isabella might someday be an old lady languishing at a nursing home with no one to love her, and I pleaded with God Our Father, His Holy Son, the Virgin Mary and all saints and angels and fortune tellers and gurus and duck hunters: please, not my baby.

Back at my desk, I sat zombie-like, watching the first brown drips slide into the glass pot. The coffee dripped faster and faster into a forced stream, and as I imagined the relief of the filter as it lightened, three sorority girls appeared, a blaze of blonde laughter, citrusy perfume and ball caps. They traced their fingers along the list of classes posted on the door. Stay the hell away from the humanities, I thought. Try engineering, think pre-med, marry a millionaire. I envisioned Isabella looking around Sherry Kinnersley's living room for me, her baby owl-eyes terrified.

The goddamn health insurance! I wouldn't have returned to work, but I feared being without coverage: I couldn't risk showing up at the pediatrician's with a medical card and having Isabella receive the condescending care reserved for the poor.

"Greetings to the new madre," Ray Dobbs boomed from the hallway. In one hand he held his prized Iliad coffee mug, in the other—oh, my despairing heart—was a plastic vase of flag-red carnations. He cut through the sorority girls, offering each a gallant, lecherous bow, and placed the flowers on my desk.

"Ain't that sweet," Diane called from her side of the office, her sarcasm loaded with depressing, misbegotten jealously

"Pretty," I said.

"Not half so pretty as you m'dear," Ray said, staring at my wet shirt.

Jesus, how could I bear the sight of him—sleep crusties lodged in the corners of his rheumy eyes, a puff of chest hair cresting like meringue over the top of his V-neck sweater, khakis jacked up to his breast bone—when I was used to looking at the singularly lovely Isabella?

After he got his coffee and moon-walked out of the office, I opened the bottom drawer for the auxiliary box of Kleenex. Taped to the box was a laminated saint card featuring a starlet-pretty woman in a flowing white robe. Above her head, the wind-blown banner read: Saint Anne, Patron Saint of Mothers. I unstuck the card from the box, studying Saint Anne's rouged, beatific face. Her velvety red mouth was puckered into a kissing smile, and I wondered if Isabella held the memory of my morning kisses, or if she ached with abandonment. Saint Anne nodded ever so slightly. I held the prayer card closer to my face and saw creases of worry ruining her high forehead, her smile fading to a grim line. She raised her hand to me, offering comfort from beyond the plastic veneer, opened her doll's mouth and said. "Isabella needs you. You must go to her."

I remember grabbing my back pack and running out of the office and down the hall with one arm pressed over my breasts to prevent the slightest, excruciating bounce. But I don't remember a wash of winter sunlight as I pulled open the heavy doors of the Humanities building, don't remember car keys jangling in my hand or paying the parking lot attendant. I seemed to have been borne across town on a wave of fevered anxiety, arriving at Sherry Kinnersley's house with my breath loud as lightning cracks, my heart drumming in all my joints. I don't remember walking through the front door, but I will never forget seeing Isabella slumped in a mechanical baby swing, sobbing, the to-and fro of the swing a tell-tale heart pounding there in Sherry Kinnersley's living room. I grabbed Isabella out of the swing—Did I unfasten a safety strap?—and felt her body relax into mine, crushing me with heavy love, and I remember whispering "home," and that a fat baby boy parked in a play pen stretched his arms up, bobbing his teary, apple-red face at me. I remember that, as I opened the door, Sherry Kinnersley appeared, saying I needed to knock before I came in, that her home was her workplace or some such bullshit, and that, later, I regretted leaving behind a pack of Huggies Supremes and a lilac quilt. And I have a cinematically precise memory of sitting in the front seat of my car, breast feeding Isabella, popping in the Mozart cassette to develop her brain, staring out the window at the bare-branched trees, unable to look at my baby for fear of finding a bruise on her body, the idea of someone hurting Isabella a fear that animated my pre-motherhood fears into fat, inconsequential bluebirds that tweet-tweeted with sweet cartoon mouths: Bye-Bye!

I remember buckling Isabella into her car seat and driving cautiously to our home.

That afternoon I sat on a park bench with Isabella snuggled next to my heart in her baby carrier, breast feeding. It was early December but the air was October-crisp and carried the sweet, raisin pie smell of pot smoke. I looked around for the suspects— the goth teenagers wearing geisha make-up, the hippie parents by the duck pond?—and spotted two girls popping out from under the jungle gym, spacy-eyed and giggling. Eleven, maybe

twelve, they wore unbuttoned black cardigans over tight mid-
riffs—possibly bikini tops—and their stomachs shimmered with
gold glitter. I gave the girls a stern look as they clomped past in
their huge shoes, oblivious. The idea that Isabella's infanthood
might be the easy part made me want to race to the store for
five thousand cartons of cigarettes and doughnuts, but I had a
new-found, fanatical faith in the future. I had experienced true
religious visitation, not the head of Jesus forming sketchily in a
cumulous crowd, delighting me with a dramatic reading of
Prince's "Raspberry Beret" or Agnes, patron saint of girls, skimming the ceiling of my sophomore biology class as she lectured
on the merits of girl power, not even the Virgin Mary appearing to me later that same year at my mother's funeral, kneeling
next to me in the pew and kissing my fingertips before she
walked back to her usual spot next to the altar—stiffer with
each step, her soft lips turning ceramic—and resumed her
statued self. The patron saint of mothers had addressed me spe-
cifically and instructionally, perhaps miraculously.

When Isabella stopped feeding I propped her up and
pointed out the bucket swings for babies—soon, I promised,
soon—and the space ship slide, where a mother and father and
their little girl lumbered up the ladder like The Three Bears—
mama bear first, baby bear in the middle, then papa bear. The
parents emanated a certain sporty wholesomeness: church goers
who drank beer in moderation, they took their daughter to the
natural history museum and bought her fanciful animal masks
in the gift shop; they fed her organic milk and vegetables, and,

not being fanatical, Doritos and Frosted Flakes. The little girl would remember her first years collaged with the Teletubbies and inflatable pool rings and love and cup cakes and the Zoo and the space ship slide and love, and love. The authenticity of this happy family, real or imagined, made me sick. I kissed Isabella on her spindly monkey fingers, saying: *Oh, sugar pop, my beautiful bat, my scary canary, I'm sorry.* At 29 I'd gotten pregnant, my own divine mystery: the condom didn't break, and I was on the pill. Had the Double Dutch method ever been known to fail? I never told the donorfather: I didn't want my baby subjected to visits with his anorexic British wife glaring at the little love child, didn't want a weird mother-in-law to show up and whisk my baby off to bible camp. But being a cool, single mom—that nine-month dream of hypothetical hipness—was easier with an in-utero baby. Now I ached with the certainty that Isabella would one day look at the fathers at the playground swinging their children higher than mothers ever swing their children, and she would feel her loss amplified as the swinging children arced up, and up, their feet piercing the clouds. Then I cheered myself by thinking that even if I'd married and planned my pregnancy, I would have chosen a loser and Isabella and I—Just the two of us! Building rainbows in the sky!—were better off as a duo. Hooray! But how I wished Isabella could have the perfect nuclear family, a biosphere of joy, a man to bring home the bacon. I would be more than willing to fry it up in the pan.

But far worse than the happy bears on the space ship slide was the trio approaching: a grandmother, a mother and a baby. The grandmother held the baby, while the mother, who looked to be about my age, ate a chocolate bar. I heard only fragments of the mother's complaints: "so fucking tired," "fat," and "vacuuming;" but the grandmother's voice boomed out, stabbing me with it's kindness: "Oh, honey, I know."

They slowed as they walked past me, smiling, wanting to talk about the matching pink hats their baby and Isabella were wearing—Hanna Anderson! Too expensive, but can you believe that soft cotton—so I pulled Isabella close and ignored them, wishing for roughly the billionth time that my own mother were still alive, to listen to me whine, to love me. And since Isabella's birth and my discovery of the hardships of maternal love, I'd worried about my mother. I hoped the claim that your life flashed before your eyes in the seconds preceding death wasn't true, that my mother's final seconds in the crashing van didn't include a fast photo montage of our life together, followed by the realization she was leaving me.

On the walk home I heard a ding! ding! ding! and, forgetting the season, dug in my pocket for change to buy a bomb pop or a clown sundae, but it was only wind chimes jangling above a blue door.

Sometimes I would see dense-looking redneck chicks and marvel at their scrubbed babies, because bathing Isabella was a challenge. That night I anchored the baby bath tub over the kitchen sink as I rocked Isabella in one arm. I filled the tub and dropped in the floating duck thermometer, adjusting the cold and hot water until I measured a perfect 98 degrees. By the time I undressed Isabella, the water cooled, and so I added more hot water, making it too hot, and little nude Isabella started to cry so I wrapped her in a fluffy towel still warm from the dryer, and she peed, so I had to get a new, un-warmed towel from the laundry basket, and then adjust the water again and again, before I eased her into the tub. As I washed her red-blonde hair, Isabella gazed at the bottle of golden shampoo on the counter, and at the canisters filled with coffee and macaroni and sugar. Happiness swelled in me like a dippy song; she was my brown-eyed girl. I draped the washcloth over her stomach, the dearest baby tube top, and rinsed her off.

After I diapered and dressed Isabella, we nestled on the couch, blissing out, breast feeding. Then, the terror of the doorbell. I rose up with Isabella still latched on and tiptoed to the door. She popped off my nipple with a howl as I looked out the peep hole and saw Ray Dobbs, wild-haired as a yak, rocking back and forth in jogging shoes.

Relieved not to find some dangerous stranger parading as a Jehovah's witness, guns and hunting knives lining his trench coat, I unlocked the door and opened it.

"A very fine evening to you, m'lady and child," said Ray Dobbs. He tried to bow but lost his footing. "I hope you don't mind me stopping by. I found your address in the staff directory."

"Well, Jesus. Are you drunk?"

He started to recite a dirty limerick about Veronica and a gin and tonica, but I said I couldn't leave the door open or Isabella would get cold. So Ray Dobbs stumbled in, rubbing his hands together as if anticipating a fine turkey dinner. He plopped down on my Venus fly trap of a couch, which swallowed up the midsection of his body, leaving his head, hands and jogging shoes floating there beyond the brown corduroy.

"She's a beautiful baby," Ray Dobbs said, though Isabella's rosebud face was scrunched on my shoulder.

"I know."

He looked around my one-bedroom house: the old carpet and junk-shop furniture and the bright new baby gear: bassinet, Diaper Genie, changing table, toys, clothes, car seat, vibrating chair. After sorting through the books on the coffee table, (Drs. Seuss and Sears) he inhaled dramatically and addressed the Holstein cow dangling on a mobile over his head: "Diane said you jumped ship this morning."

"I'm quitting; I can't be away from my baby."

"Do you have your financial plans . . . planned?"

"Not exactly, no."

"I was wondering if we might help each other out," he said, still staring up at the cow. "I could pay you quite handsomely to be my companion."

Maybe it was because I had on a plaid night gown and fuzzy socks, but I thought he wanted an assistant, some zany Gal Friday to take Christmas shopping. I envisioned myself at the cosmetic counter at Penneys, deciding between lilac or lily-of-the-valley talcum powder for his elderly sister while Ray Dobbs ogled the grossed-out sales girl.

Slowly, my brain connected the dots.

"You want me to be your companion, Ray? Your companion-companion?"

"I've always found you most fetching." He snaked out his tongue and looked at me, licking his chapped lips. "Most fetching. How much money would you need to alleviate your most pressing burdens?"

I thought about having him arrested for solicitation; I thought about Isabella plunked in the swing at Sherry Kinnersley's house.

"Eighteen hundred dollars a month," I said.

"That sounds fine. I have significant savings," he said, tripping over the s's.

And so there it was. Relief rang in my body like Christmas bells, though my nerves felt garlanded with silver tinsel. I could pay my rent, bills and health insurance cobra. I enjoyed my moment of martyrdom before remembering the faux leopard coat and hat I'd seen on the sale rack at Baby Gap: Should I gamble and wait for the second markdown? How soon could I expect payment from Ray Dobbs?

He propelled himself off the sofa on his third try, tipping an invisible hat. "May I visit you on Tuesdays, Thursdays, and Sundays at approximately this time?"

"Fine," I said, and led him to the door, already thinking he was wasting my time on a Monday night.

"I bid you—" he said, just as Isabella turtled her head up off my neck and started to cry.

"Bye, Ray." I banged the door shut.

I turned on the radio, needing a blaring pop song to distract me from the stark freakiness of my encounter with Ray Dobbs, and the serious grotesquerie on deck. I danced around the living room, held in some curious star shower of maternal ecstasy, until Isabella fell asleep on my shoulder, until I felt hollowed and loopy with fatigue and crashed on the couch to watch Entertainment Tonight.

Isabella pooped and peed. She watched blackbirds dreamily; she napped and snacked. I changed diapers and did laundry and breastfed Isabella and daydreamed of Saint Anne at the park and at the grocery store, and then it was night all over again, with the doorbell ringing, with me staring out at Ray Dobbs, who stood on the concrete porch holding a shopping bag and a bottle of wine, the year's first snow flakes clinging to his dark coat like intense dandruff. I felt unrescued and afraid, but blessed to have spent the day with Isabella, so I soldiered through, opening the door with a game, porno grin.

"Hi, Ray. I'll have to get Isabella to sleep first."

"Don't keep me waiting too long," said Hefner of the Humanities with a wink.

I pointed him to the bedroom, then gently laid Isabella in a bassinet outside the bedroom door. She screeched in surprise, accustomed as she was to sleeping cuddled next to me, but I whisper-sang to her, patting her tummy until she could not fight sleep. I switched on the baby monitor and placed it next to the bassinet, then walked into the bedroom and shut the door.

Ray had flung his jacket and shirt over the rocking chair, and stuck the bottle of wine in the chairs' cushioned seat between a stuffed zebra and a pacifier. I stared, mesmerized by the incongruity of that, by Ray Dobbs relaxing in my bedroom in black tuxedo pants and a wife beater T-shirt.

I flipped on the baby monitor receiver on my night stand. He picked up the wine.

"Could you give me a corkscrew?" He winked. "Or possibly a cockscrew?"

I shook my sad, shocked head; I did not own a corkscrew.

Ray put the wine back on the chair and sang one bright verse. "If you haven't got a corkscrew a cockscrew will do, if you haven't got a cockscrew then God bless you."

As he handed me the shopping bag I comforted myself with the novena from my childbirth class—breathe deep and relax—and pulled out an orange night gown with a yellow bodice and a strip of sheer white at the bust, like candy corn. I pulled off my sweat pants and my sweat shirt. Ray Dobbs was going to be out of my house in 15 minutes, tops.

"It's probably too small," I said. "I'm still fat from my pregnancy."

"Ah, yes," he said, nodding at my bra with industrial-sized straps and my fat- grandma underpants.

It occurred to me that he didn't sleep with his students.

"Do you feel wicked?" Ray asked, licking his index finger.

"What?" I asked, wincing, hoping to shame him, but he repeated the question with equal moxie. It seemed he was not, after all, a nebbish, fruity old professor looking to alleviate his horny loneliness; he wanted not just bang for his buck, but degradation. I turned away, trying to compress my body as I took off my bra and underpants. The nightgown smelled cheaply of tires and discount stores; I held my breath as I yanked it over my head.

"You're a sexy one," he said as I faced him again. Jesus, Mary, and Joseph, Ray Dobbs was nude as a bald eagle. He grabbed me with shaking hands—I recalled his trembly signature on class rosters—and blurted, "I brought rubbers."

Rubbers! The malt-shoppe ring of it! I'd come of age in the time of HIV, and only heard condoms called rubbers in movies and books. If only a boy named Johnny would pull up in his convertible and take me to the drive-in: the slap of the screen door, the crunch-crunch of gravel beneath my saddle shoes as I raced down the driveway of my white farm house, the wind whipping my pony tail, the leather upholstery creaking as I hopped in the car, as he leaned over to kiss my perfumed ear and whisper, "I brought rubbers." Oh, Johnny!

Ray Dobbs pulled me down on my bed. Beneath his piney cologne he smelled rotted as books in a wet basement. I closed my eyes, trying to will my senses into hibernation, and my plaid-uniformed high school self appeared, flickering willy-nilly beneath my lids, racing down corridor after corridor, searching for the library. When he tried to touch my breast I slapped away his hand—the thought of Isabella being exposed to his old man germs!

"Under no circumstances will I raise this nightgown above my waist," I said, as if that was a known rule.

Ray Dobbs muttered" you're a meanie," and his front dentures popped out with a chicken-bone snap. He slurped them back up to the gum line with his tongue, then struggled around with the condom—the rubber—and plunged his old body into mine. I gasped, shocked by the dry, shredding pain that dulled labor to a scratch, by Ray Dobbs, who didn't, at the final second, reveal a heart of gold.

"Oh you feel so good, so goddamn good," he said, his vocal inflections matching his thrusting, and then a woman's voice said, "Sweetie, for the love of Christ, what were you thinking when you agreed to this?"

I unclenched my eyes and saw her sitting on the edge of my bed, smoking. She'd aged since her starlet era documented on the prayer card—her luminous face had fallen into a constellation of wrinkles, freckles and age spots, and white skunk stripes wound through her long black hair.

She had not forgotten me.

"Oh, thank you," I cried, dissolving from the lavish miracle of Saint Anne—behold, the mother of the handmaiden of the Lord—appearing again .

"I think I might be sick," Saint Anne said, scooting to the edge of the bed, shading her eyes to block the view of Ray Dobb's wide bottom flapping up and down. "I certainly don't think this is the answer, angel."

Did she not know the pain I was in? How I worried my episiotimy would split?

"But you're the one guiding me," I said. "If you could have seen Isabella strapped in that swing."

She took a drag off her cigarette and blew out smoke rings, sending odorless halos above her head. "A smart girl like you can figure something else out."

Then Ray Dobbs, Homer scholar and naysayer of popular culture, yelled out, "Who's your daddy?"

My heart and body ached from the oddity of his words, from Saint Anne scolding me from the side of the bed, and from Isabella, who gurgled like a lonely seagull, a sound I heard in mono from behind the door and the baby monitor.

"Jesus, will things always be like this," I said, meaning my see-sawing despair and happiness, happiness and despair.

"Well, things won't always be exactly like this," Saint Anne said, good-humored now, cocking an eyebrow at Ray Dobbs. She rubbed my feet and that helped with the pain as I waited for a revelation that would solve my problems

"What can I tell you? It's hard to be a mother. For my daughter, I prayed for a peaceful life, free of drama, for Mary to never know a blue day, and look what happened: A hard birth in a stable, blood in the straw, bits of straw clinging to the vernum on baby Jesus' head, and no one to help Mary except her old husband, and then, my God! Visitors! Camels and lambs! The wise men kneeling to adore the baby. And Mary in shock that the savior was crying and colicky and wanted to nurse constantly and that she was still bleeding from the delivery. And my poor girl didn't have a goddamn clue about what she was in for."

Jesus on the cross. Those dark hours I'd spent at the Humanities office magnified two trillion times and shot to the moon could not touch the despair Mary must have felt looking at her own baby with nails pounded through his human hands—nails!—could not touch the despair of Saint Anne, who had to watch her own baby's suffering. I thought of the stone statue of Mary at church—her smile peaceful yet ironic, as if on the verge of opening her mouth and saying: I really wanted my son to live. I don't especially care what happens to any of you bastards." But she did care, she had appeared to me at my mother's funeral, dazzling me from my hard sorrows; possibly she sent her own mother to watch over me now. Or was Anne guiding everything? Did the soul of the mother ascend to heaven, or did it live forever in the daughter, lingering there in a purgatory of unconditional love?

"My Mary," Saint Anne said. "Even now I suffer for her suffering. Late at night I whisper her name over and over to myself: Mary, Mary, Mary. My only prayer."

But I was only half-listening; my thoughts drifted mossily, grandiose: Perhaps Isabella was the second coming of Christ and Saint Anne was guiding me, telling me not to let my baby suffer as saviors do, and I certainly would not allow Isabella to save the world and lose herself, though I loved the sound of Southern Baptist Isabellians. Fundamentalist Isabellians and Catholic Isabellians. The Sacred Heart of Isabella!

Ray Dobb's huffed there on top of me, saying, "you're my bitch, you're my bitch."

"How pornography teaches men to be betters lovers," Saint Anne said acidly. "Lesson One: Say 'you're my bitch' a lot. It's so attractive. And here's Lesson Two, which has nothing to with Ray Dobbs or pornography: These days with your baby are ephemeral. The fatigue, the dirty diapers, the mood swings—yours and hers—and the heaps of laundry won't last. You're dealing with an awful lot of solid matter—poop, spit-up, breast pumps, soft packs of diapers—that offers you the illusion of permanence. But soon Isabella will run through the house, her babyhood a memory. And then she'll be an adult with her own baby, and you'll grow old and you'll die. Then Isabella will grow old and die and her baby—"

"Jesus! Not Isabella!" I couldn't bear the thought of my baby dying, even if she lived to be 95. It didn't occur to me that your child growing into old age before she died was the zenith, the dream.

"Even Isabella. But it's okay." She took a deep breath and said, "Your job is to teach Isabella that God has her in his sight, to teach her that heaven exists beyond the trees and the birds and the sky." Her sudden kindergarten evangelicalism annoyed me, but she interrupted herself, resuming her regular voice: "Oh my God, Mary used to point her crooked little finger at the sky and say 'ky! ky!' and at the trees and say 'twee! twee!' Can you beat that? Can you? Ky! Twee!"

I could beat that. My twelve week old baby had, just that morning, looked at the falling snow and said "shhhhs," the very sound of snow flakes slipping onto blades of grass. But I smiled at Saint Anne's ky and twee story, as if in awe. That was the game.

"Adorable," I said.

"Anyway," Saint Anne whispered, looking down at her hands. Then she raised her hands in the air piously, assumed a saintly, beatific smile, and proclaimed, brightly: "*And Those that are hunted /Know this as their life, /Their reward: to walk /Under such trees in full knowledge /Of what is in glory above of them, /And to feel no fear, /But acceptance, compliance, /Fulfilling themselves without pain.*"

It was the middle of James Dickey's poem, "The Heaven of Animals," a big and super consolation if you were a college girl mourning Giggles the cat, but a terror when considering the mortality of a baby, of your baby.

"Oh yes, here we are," Ray moaned.

Saint Anne raised her hands higher in the air—Hallelujah Jesus, Ray Dobbs, and James Dickey!—but her bottom lip trembled, and when she spoke again her voice sounded ragged, wasted from years and years of crying and smoking: "*At the cycle's center, /They tremble, they walk /Under the tree, / They fall, they*" *are torn, / They rise, they walk again."*

Ray Dobbs rolled away from me whispering, "Well, well, well" and I jumped out of bed and wrapped myself in my robe. Although I felt hatcheted in every way, no blood dripped down my legs and the room looked unsplattered except for one dark red spot, a Rorschach rose blooming on the white sheet. I opened the bedroom door, picked Isabella out of the bassinet, and told her I loved her.

When I looked back I saw Saint Anne stubbing out her cigarette on the window sill. As Ray Dobbs dressed, she scurried around, stripping the bed. She bundled up the skanky sex sheets and jammed them in the clothes basket, then made up the bed with my blue flannel sheets; Ray Dobbs counted out six soft twenties and placed them on my dresser.

"I'll go now," he said in a repentant, rehearsed voice. He didn't notice Saint Anne placing a foil-wrapped mint on my pillow, didn't notice her slipping out the door with him, or that she turned back around and touched my forehead, then Isabella's.

"There's one more thing I need to tell you," she said, her face a mask of solemnity before it collapsed, goofily, into a smile. "Your baby is beautiful."

"That's another thing you didn't have to tell me, " I said, still vexed about the poem, and that she hadn't spirited Ray Dobbs away and replaced him with a bag of rare gold coins. "But thanks."

Saint Anne kissed my lips and was gone. I shut the door and stood at the front window, watching her walk down the street. I expected her to evanesce into dust or snow flakes, but she followed Ray Dobbs down the block as he walked down the street and got into his car. Then I saw her look over at a nativity scene on a lawn across the street. Lit from within by neon bulbs, all the holy players had an early eighties, new-wave glow—if resurrected they might eschew religious dogma, douse themselves in eyeliner and sing: I'll tumble for ya!—and the three wise men—Wise! Men!—loomed twice the size of Mary. I thought Saint Anne might run up in the lawn and give the wise men a good kick, but she kept going, walking into the darkness under the broken-out streetlights at the end of the block, disappearing.

I looked out the window for a long time, and when Isabella woke, she peered out, too, mesmerized by the Christmas lights strung on the houses across the street, candy-bright against the black sky, and by the glowing nativity scene. Saint Anne must have looked at the neon rendition of Mary and remembered holding her daughter to her heart—the distilled sunshine and snow smell of a clean baby, the tiny feet tucking around her ribs—and wanted those first days back, before the Archangel Gabriel appeared, before the suffering of Jesus, and her daughter's exalted eternity. I didn't think I would ever be that mother looking across the street, wounded by fate and poetry, thinking: come back, come back. I believed, fanatically,

that Isabella and I would always be there at the window together, even as I mourned for my own mother, imagined her
not dead all these long years, but alive and recovering from
amnesia, some debilitating amnesia that had led her away from
me, imagined her the driver of the blue Ford coming down
the street—headlights blasting the darkness, the radio pumping out a rap song muted by the hush of falling snow. As the
car passed under the streetlight in front my house, I held Isabella
closer to the window. "Mom," I whispered, "look at my baby."

I felt so alive with hurt and wonder that I wanted to smash
my head through the window and feel glass and cold air slice
my face. Instead, I kissed my baby's tender, pulsing head. *Isabella*,
I whispered, the beauty of that word a perpetual comfort, an
astonishment. Why would anyone name a baby anything else?
Isabella, Isabella, Isabella, Isabella . . .